About the Author

Dan Elish co-wrote the book to the Broadway musical *13*, which has been performed all over the world and is now a movie on Netflix. He is also the book writer and co-lyricist to Off Broadway's *The Evolution of Mann*. Additionally, he is the author of twelve novels for readers of all ages, including *The Worldwide Dessert Contest, Nine Wives,* and *Born Too Short,* which won an International Reading Association Students' Choice Award for young adult literature. Dan lives in New York City with his wife and two children.

3/19/25

King of Broadway

Hi Teale,

I hope this book

makes you smile—

Thanks,

Dan

Dan Elish

King of Broadway

Olympia Publishers
London

www.olympiapublishers.com
OLYMPIA PAPERBACK EDITION

A CIP catalogue record for this title is
available from the British Library.

ISBN: 978-1-83543-244-0

This is a work of fiction.
Names, characters, places and incidents originate from the writer's
imagination. Any resemblance to actual persons, living or dead, is
purely coincidental.

First Published in 2024

Olympia Publishers
Tallis House
2 Tallis Street
London
EC4Y 0AB

Printed in Great Britain

Dedication

For anyone who has ever written a musical.

Acknowledgments

Many thanks to friends and family who read drafts of *King of Broadway* along the way. As seems to always be the case, I could not have finished the book without the encouragement and advice of the brilliant John Canaday. Also, major props and thanks to my fine agent Matt Bialer and his assistant Bailey Tamayo. Other good friends read drafts, and I thank them all for their time and excellent advice: Peter Benson, Matthew Gartner, Dave Hill, Billy Aronson, Chuck Lane, Eric Weiner, Doug Cohen, Irwin Appel, Betsy Hickok and Leslie Pietrzyk. Major thanks, too, to my ultra-supportive family who read and encouraged along the way: Herb (my dad), Harry (my brother), Andrea (beloved wife), and Cassie and John Elish (fabulous children). Finally, many thanks to all my musical theater attending and writing friends—many of whom I have known for years now all of whom helped inspire this book.

1

The great man stood in the half-opened doorway, as rumpled as in all the pictures. His blue cardigan hung loosely off his shoulders, and his famous beard, long and white, made Ben wonder if he was really face to face with possibly the greatest musical theater composer of his generation or if Santa had come to New York for vacation.

"So here you are. The young fellow who wrote me."

Ben swallowed.

"Yes, Mr. King. It's me."

The old man scratched his side and swung the door all the way open.

"All right then," he said with a sigh. He waved vaguely toward the living room. "In you go."

With that, Ben stepped into his idol's house, really the idol of every young composer/lyricist in the city. Heart pounding, he followed the shuffling icon into his very own living room.

"I get a lot of these letters," King began with a grunt as he planted himself into an easy chair. No formalities, it seemed. "Usually young, nice-looking people wanting to get a little glimmer of advice from the withered genius. They say Sondheim used to answer every single one. How in the world did he do that? I try to meet with who I can. But you? Advice isn't enough, is it? You came right out and sent me your book. Wanting me to help you turn it into a musical."

Ben was now on a plush red sofa, face to face with the man

whose picture he had seen in everything from the *Times* to coffee table books on the history of Broadway. He looked older now, of course – that happened even to the astonishingly brilliant. But despite the expected wrinkles and very slight stoop, he was a young eighty-five.

"Yes," Ben said. "A children's novel. *The Worldwide Dessert Contest.*"

They both glanced at the copy that Ben had sent, face up on the coffee table. Horatio King picked it up and examined the cover, a picture of a forty-year-old dessert chef and a little girl, his faithful assistant, surrounded by a squadron of apple pies on roller-skates.

"By Ben Willis," King said.

"Right," the young man replied with an embarrassed laugh.

Just then, a white poodle sprung seemingly out of nowhere and began to lick the small sections of King's face not covered by his beard. If Ben expected King to be affectionate with a beloved pet, he was mistaken. The winner of eight Tony Awards gave the dog a cursory pat, then shoved him to the floor.

"Piss off, Juniper."

Apparently used to such treatment, the dog scurried away happily enough. King tossed the book back to the table, then stood up. Despite the reliance on a cane, Ben was impressed by how well he moved for a man of his years.

"You want to turn your little epic into a show, do you?" King paced toward a fireplace–a luxury in Manhattan that gave the elegant living room the feel of a country inn.

"That's the hope," Ben said. "I'm in the AMI workshop now."

King shuddered.

"The AMI workshop?"

"Um, yes. The American Musical Theater Institute. You know it?"

A stupid question. No, a moronic one. Of course, Horatio King knew it. But Ben couldn't have anticipated what came next.

"Workshops are shit," the great man intoned. "No place to learn the craft. Is it still run by Ethan Hancock?"

Ben nodded. "It is."

"A hack," King intoned. "Why in fuck's name are you in such a thing?"

Ben swallowed hard. He had been warned about King's notorious mouth, but to hear his icon cursing out loud – especially when he was nothing but polite in interviews – was a shock.

"Because I was accepted, I guess," Ben stammered. His heart was suddenly beating like it was attached to a malfunctioning pacemaker. "I wrote two musicals in college."

If King was impressed with that fact – one Ben had been waiting to drop – he didn't show it.

"Of course you did," King said. "Every young composer who begs to meet me wrote two musicals in college. Never one. Never three. Always two." He was pacing now, pushing his cane wildly in front of him, planting it on the rug. "The AMI workshop, huh? Let me guess how it's gone. First, they told you to write an "I Want" song where your hero declares that his life would be perfect if he could bone a Playboy Bunny. Then they told you to write a Charm Song where the Playboy Bunny and your hero realize that they want to walk the Adirondack Trail dressed as nuns. And then – yes, I know – they told you to take some impossible, ridiculous thing – something like Jay Gatsby's death – yes, that's it! – turn the end of *The Great Gatsby* into a musical scene. Am I right? Is that what you had to do?"

Ben's heart was still pounding. By that point, King was next to him on the sofa, looking him square in the eye.

"Something like that," Ben said. "We do assignments but we also write our own shows."

King grunted and picked a piece of lint off of his pants. "And thus your presence here today. The book you want to turn into a musical. Your cookbook?"

"No, no," Ben said. "*The Worldwide Dessert Contest*. It's fiction."

Ben was beginning to see why the old man hadn't written in fifteen years. The famous temper. The mood swings. Rumors of alcohol. Drugs, prescribed and not. He had been this way since his last failure, a musical based on the movie *Black Hawk Down*. Word on the Rialto was that King had never recovered. At least, he hadn't written since.

"Well, you're here," King said. "So come on then. Tell me the plot."

"The plot?" Ben asked.

For some reason he hadn't been prepared to tell the story point by point. Stupidly, Ben had thought that King would've skimmed the *Publisher's Weekly* review he had included in the package he had sent, which gave a brief synopsis of the book and then raved, "Call this a kids' librarian's dream."

"You know the plot, I presume?"

"Of course I do."

"Then tell me the goddamn thing!"

What choice did Ben have? He drew in a deep breath. He told him the goddamn thing.

"Well, it's about this guy named John Applefeller, a dessert chef. He's forty and every year he and his ten-year-old assistant, Samantha, want to win The Worldwide Dessert Contest. Except there's a problem. Applefeller's desserts always change into other things."

King raised an eyebrow.

"Change into other things?"

"Why yes."

"What things?"

Ben forged on. "One year his apple soufflé puffs up into a giant balloon."

King wrinkled his already rather wrinkled brow. "Repeat that."

Ben was terrified – suddenly the plot he had worked on for years sounded irredeemably stupid.

"His apple soufflé puffs up into a giant balloon."

King looked confused. "That's supposed to be funny?"

"Well, yes. Then his Apple French Toast turns into kneepads."

King scoffed. "Kneepads?"

"Yes. Which he sells to the United States Olympic Team."

"And this is a musical?" King asked. "A musical that you have the temerity to ask me to write with you?"

Before Ben could appropriately respond his idol stormed on. "What do you plan for an opening number?"

"What?"

"An opening number?" King growled. "What is it?"

"I've written a lyric. It's called 'The Man with the Changing Desserts.'"

King snorted. "*You've* written the lyrics? What do you need me for then?"

It was a valid question. In truth, Ben had sent the book mostly as an excuse to meet the great man with the absurd hope that King would fall in love with the story and offer to collaborate.

"They're just a start," Ben said.

"Okay, okay," King said. Something Ben hardly dared hope was interest shone in the man's eyes. "So we have John Applefeller, a maker of changing desserts, and his kid assistant, Samantha, did I hear that right?"

"Yes. And every year Applefeller wants to win The Worldwide Dessert Contest. But every year he comes in last, you know, because his desserts always change. And in the process, the changing desserts hurt the head judge in some way."

King raised another eyebrow. Ben couldn't decide if he really was interested or just too lazy or old to throw him out.

"The head judge is Nathaniel Barkle," Ben went on.

"And he's the one who gets hurt by Applefeller's desserts?"

"Right."

At least the old man was following the plot.

"How does he get hurt?"

"All different ways," Ben said. "But mainly there's the time when the caramel in a batch of Applefeller's caramel apples change into the world's most powerful glue. The apple brushes against Barkle's face and sticks there."

"Sticks there?" King sputtered. "For how long? A day?"

He pushed Juniper away again, this time with a terse, "Fuck off."

"For his whole life," Ben said.

King looked him square in eye. For the first time, the young man was convinced he had his full attention.

"What are you telling me?" he said with the hint of a smile. "He goes through his life with a giant caramel apple stuck to his face?"

"Yes," Ben said. "Right on the side of his cheek."

To Ben's shock, King broke into a large smile, displaying a row of small yet perfectly proportional white teeth. He stroked his beard.

"*Hmmm*," he said. "A caramel apple on his face."

"Right," Ben said, perhaps too enthusiastically. "That's the name of one of the songs."

King frowned again.

"Sounds like you've written the whole damned thing."

"No, no," Ben said. "Only parts of it." He gulped and plunged ahead. "I need a collaborator."

"And you came to me, eh? Pretty ballsy, don't you think? You honestly think I'd be interested in collaborating with a child? I'm Horatio King. You're little Ben Willis from God knows where."

It was true. Ben's letter had been presumptuous and more than a little bit crazy. In the way of these spur-of-the-moment risks, Ben had written the great man late one night with the prodding of his roommate, Harrison. Also, in the way of such things, Ben had been seriously drunk.

"It's true." Ben's voice trailed off. "But you know. Nothing ventured."

King waved him off, lurching back around the room. For an old man, he liked to move. "I must be just that bored, but now my interest is piqued. What happens next in your little tale of intrigue?"

"In the story?"

"Yes, your dessert opus! What's next?"

Ben spoke quickly.

"The year the story begins, Applefeller enters the world's largest apple pancake. But when it comes time to taste his dessert, it turns into a giant trampoline."

"Trampoline? The pancake?"

"Right."

King grunted in apparent disbelief. Ben rushed through the rest of it before the old man could change his mind.

"The bad guy is Sylvester Sweet, and his pet elephant – his name is Tuba – head butts Judge Barkle onto the apple-pancake trampoline, and he bounces hundreds of feet into the air, screaming like a maniac. That's when the janitor of the contest, this old–timer named Josiah Benson, tells Applefeller about a chef named Captain B. Rollie Ragoon, who knows how to make magical desserts – he lives in a land called Iambia, where everyone speaks only in rhymes."

"Rhymes!"

"Right. Rhymes. That's one of the reasons I thought it could make a good musical."

King grunted again. "Continue."

Ben didn't wait for further encouragement. "The Ragoon tells Applefeller the plan to take on Sylvester Sweet at the next year's contest with roller-skating apple pies. But Sweet steals the roller-skating pies, and the Ragoon and Applefeller enter flying apple pies at the last minute. In the end, everything goes crazy, and Applefeller wins with a simple apple pie that Samantha brought for lunch."

Ben couldn't tell if he had lost King or not. But at the mention of the simple apple pie, King raised an eyebrow.

"So what are you telling me? After all of that nonsense with your rhyming dessert genius, Captain Rollie Lagoon…"

"Ragoon," Ben said.

"What?"

"His name. It's Captain B. Rollie Ragoon."

"Whatever," King said. "After all the shit you just recounted with roller-skating pies and flying pies, our hero wins with a simple apple pie supplied by his kid assistant? Is that what you're telling me?"

"Well, yes."

King shook his head. "No."

"What?"

"Doesn't work, that's what."

"Why?"

King waved dismissively, swatting the story away like a gnat.

"Your ending. Contrived, empty bullshit."

Ben was overwhelmed. Here he was, age twenty-five, being taken to task by the man Time Magazine had branded one of the twenty great geniuses of his era. It was all Ben could do not to crawl whimpering to the door. But genius or not, Ben knew when someone was being an asshole. And wasn't it true that assholes only respected people who talked back?

"Hold on a minute." Ben was surprised to hear the words come out of his intimidated mouth. "My editor is the best in the business."

King raised an eyebrow.

"I said that my editor…"

"My hearing aid is quite operational," Horatio snapped.

"What's this editor's name?"

"Eleanor Crumb."

"Never heard of her."

Ben was all in now. "That doesn't mean she doesn't exist. She's a big deal."

"So what?"

"So, we worked hard on the plot. The ending isn't empty bullshit, that's what!"

"That may be," King said. "But does your Eleanor Crumb write musicals?"

"Well, no," Ben said.

The next thing Ben knew, King had a certain object in his right hand. Though it was smaller than he had thought it would be, Ben knew precisely what it was: A Tony Award.

"Do you think I won one of these by writing insignificant fables about misguided dessert chefs?"

King wobbled closer to Ben, which is when the boy thought again about the tales of alcohol abuse that had followed King's career. Then he realized. Was the great man drunk now? At three in the afternoon? It was certainly possible. Because suddenly, the award was right under Ben's nose. Its spinning globe brushed against his chin.

"Best Score," King thundered.

"Yes," Ben said. "For Lear, right?"

"Of course for Lear," King said, all but lurching onto the couch next to him, nearly squashing his poodle in the process. "What the fuck else would it be? Lear is an adaption of Shakespeare! The noble Bard himself. The story of a king! Not some hopeless wannabe's preposterous drivel about a hapless wretch who makes changing desserts!"

With that, King used the Tony to point toward the door.

"What?" Ben asked.

"I knew I shouldn't have agreed to this. Consider your meeting with your idol complete. Chalk that one off your list. You have strained an old man's patience to the breaking point."

"How's that?" Ben sputtered.

"Your idea is preposterous, that's how," King cried. "What made you think I'd be interested in a musical about a maker of changing desserts?"

Ben swallowed hard. "They said you were looking for a new project."

King narrowed his eyes. "Who said?"

"People. People in my workshop."

"Ethan Hancock?"

Ben nodded. "Maybe, yes."

King's eyes went wide in horror. "Not that hack again! What could a non-talent like him know about the inner-life of a genius?" He pointed to the door. "Go, Dessert-boy. Get thee hither! Write an "I Want" song about a girl who wants to be a gay giraffe! Write a charm song about a urologically impaired dwarf! But get out! Go!"

At that point, Juniper, the erstwhile oppressed dog, got into the act, yapping wildly at Ben's feet. Making a mad dash for the front door, the young man heard something bash against the doorframe. He turned just in time to see the Tony fall to the foyer floor. Ben gasped. For an old man, Horatio King had a good arm – and good aim, too. The thing had nearly hit him in the back of the head.

2

Ben hadn't had a girlfriend for well over a year – but since college, there had always been Gretchen Todd, on-again, off-again hookup, best friend, and perennial first call. As of late, his potential future wife, too. During their most recent rendezvous, the sometimes couple had jokingly pledged to marry at forty-three and a half if they were both still single, in time for Gretchen to sneak in a baby or two under the wire. It wasn't the most romantic arrangement. Still, it gave Ben solace to know a plan was in place to stave off middle-to-old-age loneliness. Despite ambitions that included Newbery and Tony Awards – and what the hell, a Pulitzer or two – Ben was wise enough – just barely – to realize that missing out on having a family would be something to regret.

A middle-school English and Drama teacher in rural Vermont, Gretchen was driving home through the fall colors when her phone rang – a call she had been expecting.

"So?" she answered, putting Ben on speaker. He had reached for his cell the minute he hit the street. "How'd it go?"

"Let's see," Ben said. "I'm not unconscious."

"Um…Why would you be?"

Ben delivered a blow-by-blow of the meeting with their mutual idol. (Along with teaching English, Gretchen directed the annual community theater musical, including a production of one of King's early works, *Moses and Me!* based on Robert A. Caro's *The Power Broker*.) By the time he was finished with his tale of woe, Ben was crossing 5th Avenue, headed into Central Park. Even in New York City, the foliage was bright and beautiful.

"Wow," Gretchen said.

"Yeah, that's about all you could say," Ben replied. "Wow."

"So I'll say it again. Wow."

"Yeah."

"Was he drunk?"

"The thought occurred to me," Ben said, "but no. I think he's just sort of a jerk."

"Sort of a jerk?" Gretchen said. "Let me get this straight. He threw his Tony at your head?"

"I think that's where he was aiming, yes."

"He told his dog to fuck off?"

Ben was walking by the Central Park Zoo now, weaving around a group of tourists with the dexterity of a born-and-bred New Yorker – which he was. "Well, the first time he told him to 'piss off.'"

"That's not much better."

"You once told your cat to fuck off."

"That's different," Gretchen said. "My cat's insane."

Ben heard what he thought was a screech, probably Gretchen taking a country road corner at a high speed. She was a notoriously lousy driver.

"Anyway," she went on, "you've had a hell of a week."

Ben sighed.

"More like the week from hell."

Indeed, Ben's ill-fated meeting with Horatio King had been but the grand finale in a short block of time gone frustratingly awry. Perhaps even more upsetting than being driven from his idol's apartment with a flying Tony was the email that Ben had received two days previous from the famous Eleanor Crumb. The subject line of his editor's devastating missive had been the title of Ben's as-yet-unpublished second manuscript: *The Golden Television*, a children's novel about a boy who disappears into a TV-themed world where the villain is able to "cancel" whichever character gets in his way. To Ben it was the novel that, even more than *The Worldwide Dessert Contest*, would put him on the map, there to stay forever – the type of book he imagined being translated into over one hundred languages, read by children from Maine to Shanghai. A book that would cause him to be mobbed in airports, chased down the street by hordes of literary ten-year-olds. In short, that rare masterpiece that strikes a chord with the public while making the author mountains of cash.

It was all not to be. Yes, Eleanor Crumb was a gentle lady but one who didn't mince words. With customary dispatch, she had come right to the point.

Dear Ben,

I hate to disappoint, but *The Golden Television* is such a dreary read! Clearly, you wanted me to laugh, but alas…I didn't.

The Worldwide Dessert Contest remains a triumph, a sweet and funny book that I was proud to publish. Give me a call when you're ready, and we'll discuss how to move forward.

As I said, alas, alas, alas…

Best, Ellen

"How are you feeling?" Gretchen asked.

"About Crumb or King?"

"For now, about Crumb."

"Like I've been run over by street sweeper."

Accustomed to Ben's active imagination and tendency to melodrama, Gretchen moved on.

"Did you speak to her yet?"

Ben sighed. He was well into the park now, coming up to Sheep Meadow.

"I finally manned up and called yesterday."

"And? Any wiggle room?"

"Wiggle room?"

"You know, did she say you can rewrite it in some way?"

Ben emitted a sound not unlike the rueful laugh of the damned.

"Nope. She said it was pretty much unpublishable. She said I got caught up trying to do a modern *Phantom Tollbooth* and that it just didn't work. She said I should urinate on the manuscript."

"Urinate on it?"

"Not in those words precisely. But she did say I should quote: put it in a drawer."

"Ouch."

"Yeah, ouch."

"Is there any good news?"

Ben sighed. "Well, *The Worldwide Dessert Contest* hasn't done too badly. So she wants me to work on other ideas."

"Well, that's something," Gretchen said.

Ben heard another screech. He imagined a narrowly missed deer.

"You okay?" he asked.

"Just a chipmunk."

Ben didn't want to know it had been a close miss or a direct hit.

"So she still wants to publish you, right?" Gretchen went on.

"I guess," Ben said. "Not that I have any ideas."

"No ideas? Hello? The Tet Offensive?"

"The Tet Offensive?" Ben said. "For a kids' novel?"

"It was funny."

"We were stoned."

Gretchen laughed. "Maybe, but I liked it. Anyway, you'll think of something, relax."

Ben shook himself. "Have you ever seen me relaxed? Even once?"

"There's always a first time. Now tell me about the guy you crisped."

Ben was well used to Gretchen's sudden conversation shifts, a quality that had attracted him initially, then annoyed him after a time. Even so, it *was* a valid inquiry. In keeping with the rule of three, Ben had suffered another disaster that week. Not that he liked waiting tables or had any pre-conceived notions that he was anything other than terrible at it. Still, it had felt lousy to be fired. Was it his fault that he couldn't remember the list of over forty beers the pub served? Ben was a writer, damn it, not a performing seal! And yes, spilling the latte on the manager's husband had been unfortunate, but was it grounds for dismissal? Apparently.

"He's out of the ICU. He'll be fine."

"Good," Gretchen said. "So crisped hubby is going to be OK?"

"Stop calling him that. And yes, he'll be fine. It wasn't even that hot. He didn't have a single second-degree burn."

"That was good of him. And the restaurant's insurance is covering everything?"

"That's what I'm told."

"I like it. Nice."

Ben liked Gretchen for her naturally sunny disposition. Still, there were times he wanted her to share his gloom.

"Nice?" he said. "How is any of this nice?"

"Well, it's nice that the manager's husband will be okay and nice that Eleanor Crumb wants to see what else you come up with, right? It's also sort of nice that you met Horatio King. How was his health, by the way?"

"Fine, I think. He could sure wave a cane."

"Good," Gretchen said. "Now, which show was it?"

"Which show was what?"

"The Tony Award. That he threw at you?"

Ben laughed. How could he be offended? He would have wanted to have known the answer as well.

"Lear," Ben said.

"Ah, best score, around twenty, thirty years ago, I think," Gretchen said.

"Right," he said.

"And best production ever, Middlebury College."

A further irony. Ben and Gretchen had produced the show their junior spring.

"Damned straight," Gretchen said. "We killed it. So did you run off with it? The award?"

"Run off with it?" Ben cried, laughing now. "I was too busy ducking it."

"Oh, well. You could've made a fortune on eBay. You could've shown it to your AMI class the next time they ripped one of your songs."

Ben stopped short on the edge of Sheep's Meadow, so distracted by his meeting with Horatio King that he had almost forgotten.

"What time is it anyway?"

Gretchen wasn't the only one who could turn a conversation on a dime with a surprise question.

"Four ten, why?"

"Shit," Ben said. "I'm running late."

"For what?"

Ben laughed.

"The workshop," he said.

With a quick goodbye, Ben hurried to the AMI Building on 57th Street, just below Columbus Circle. For Ben had an assignment to perform that day: a charm song from *Lolita*, written with Drew Derrick, arguably the least talented person in the class. No, Ben didn't have high hopes for how the song might be received – but as long as he was destined to be skewered that day, he figured that he might has well show up on time and take it like a man.

3

Entering the AMI Building, Ben had already made the decision not to mention his meeting with Horatio King. Obviously, if a miracle had occurred and King had agreed to collaborate, Ben would have let the fact modestly slip, then cherished the looks of abject jealousy on the faces of his classmates. But given that he counted himself lucky to leave King's apartment without a major head injury, Ben followed his usual protocol: he entered the class said his hellos, then listened to other, mostly older, classmates engage in their favorite activity, ripping into the list of recently opened shows—the more successful and lucrative, the better.

Fortunately for the class, that fall had offered a treasure trove of questionable new material. First to open had been *Pip! Pip!* a musical adaptation of Dickens' *Great Expectations*, closely followed by *Whitman*, a one-man tuner about the famous poet in the final years of his life. Finally, there was Disney's latest entry into the Broadway sweepstakes, *Dalmatians!* a show that starred twenty actors creatively costumed as dogs. Though the show sported music and lyrics by British rock icon Eric Sanabelle, most critics had been disappointed by the score. Edgar Childs of the *New York Times* had noted, "Sanabelle's once powerful music has been chewed up like an old bone and reprocessed into soggy, half-masticated show tunes." Indeed, given the critical reaction, Tony mavens wondered if a young nobody named David McGuire would nudge Sir Sanabelle for best music and lyrics for his show, *The Evolution of Mann*, a comic musical about a young man's quest for personal growth that was slated to open that winter.

As usual, the first to hold court in the pre-class bull session was Johnny Framingham, a gay man who sported a closely cropped gray beard and a cane to offset a mild case of plantar fasciitis. As generous as he could be cutting, his favorite two subjects were musical theater and his new vegan diet.

"The trouble with *Dalmatians*," he was saying as Ben took a seat, "isn't that it is about dogs. It's that the lyrics are for the dogs."

It was a line just funny enough to coax a mild laugh from the room. It also created an opening for gap-toothed, long-haired, Billy Hansen, a wanna-be rock star turned musical theater writer.

"What do you expect?" Billy said. "Sanabelle is a rocker, not a theater writer."

"True," Johnny replied, scratching his beard. "But my God. Did you hear some of those lines?" He shook his head and smiled, as if remembering something so egregious all a person could do was laugh at the insanity of the world. "I'm sorry," he went on, "but 'sandy beaches' and 'pleased to Meech yas' do not rhyme."

This time the twitters built to chuckles and guffaws. Not funny in virtually any other setting, at the AMI workshop, Johnny's observation was class A comedy. To his everlasting discredit, Sir Sanabelle, unschooled in the tenets of musical theater writing, had filled *Dalmatians!* with scads of false, even preposterous, rhymes. While there was a long list of errors to choose from, the worst might well have been the rock star's inexplicable juxtaposition of:

Come on, baby, be my creature.
I want to pet your sheet fur.

Alongside the fact that "creature" and "sheet fur" do not

rhyme was the matter of the couplet's utter lack of meaning. Earlier that semester, the class had spent a hilarious fifteen minutes in speculation. The best guess had come from Tiffany Holt, a frizzy-haired lyric writer and masseuse in training who sat in the front row. With research, she had discovered that, in some British neighborhoods, "sheet fur" was a euphemism for a woman's kneecaps – but Ben still had his doubts. Did that mean that Sir Sanabelle wrote a lyric suggesting that one dog wanted the other to pet its kneecaps? From any angle, it was a tough sell. While a typical theater-goer might have overlooked the strange line, the members of the AMI workshop could not forget it. With the floodgates open, the comments came fast and furious.

"Sanabelle is a joke."

"A joke is right!"

"The dude knows a total of maybe six chords."

"And always writes in A major. That's a rock 'n roll key."

"His CDs are over-rated anyway."

"*Pieces of Sanabelle*? Atrocious!"

Ben smiled, remembering. Growing up, his cousin had taped the poster of the famous CD cover on the ceiling over her bed. On it, Sanabelle was dressed as a pirate in a yellow jockstrap, standing next to what by all appearances was a drunk gorilla.

The students were leaning in toward Johnny and Billy now, sharks swarming a seriously bleeding body. With Sir Sanabelle excoriated, the class moved to other prey. Next up was an Off-Broadway offering called *Margaret and her Dad* about Harry Truman's relationship with his daughter.

"A snoozola." That was Steve Andrews, a thirty-something music director. Blessed with a superior ear, he had once impressed Ben by commenting on a fellow student's 'trenchant use of subdominants.' "The futuristic scenes with other presidents weren't even funny," he went on. "Can you imagine that, people? They couldn't get a laugh from Donald Trump! Not even the Dance of the Orange Wigs!"

Which led to Tiffany Holt recreating the great dance as best she could as the class clapped.

"So?" a voice said. "Are the savages out?"

Ben looked to his right. Sidling into a chair was Jen Rosenthal, corporate lawyer by day, lyric writer by night. Two years earlier, they had been assigned the near-impossible task of writing a ballad for Lady Macbeth. Though their resultant song was terrible, they had stayed friends.

"Yep," Ben said. "Mostly ripping into Sir Sanabelle."

Jen shrugged. "Well, he does sort of deserve it. I mean, rhyming "hickey" with "pickle" really made my skin crawl."

Ben laughed. He agreed. Still, bad rhymes and obvious chord progressions aside, it was a hit. Maybe Sir Sanabelle knew more about what the public wanted than the members of the workshop?

"Anyway," Johnny was now declaring. "I still say the best writer around now that Sondheim is gone is Horatio King."

Ben smiled.

"King?" someone asked.

"Of course," Billy replied. "His Lear is genius."

"I agree," a classmate said. "But the dude hasn't written for years."

"I hear he lives alone with a poodle, right?"

"I hear he kicks the poodle."

"I hear he drinks all day."

"No, living with King, it's the poodle that drinks."

As laughter rippled through the classroom, Ben was once again tempted to jump in and tell his story. He might have done it, too, if Ethan Hancock – the man King had called a hack – hadn't entered. He was tall and sleek with a Tony Award to his name for music and lyrics for *Stepping Out*, an upscale musical Ben had loved set in 1930s Detroit.

"Well, well, well," he intoned, sitting down. "More talk of Horatio King and his little doggie dog."

Again, it was all Ben could do not to shout out what had happened at his meeting.

"Yo, everyone! I met Horatio King! Me! He threw a Tony at my head!"

But he held his tongue. Though people in the class had been supportive of *The Worldwide Dessert Contest* – Jen and one or two others had even read it – Ben felt embarrassed to admit that he had had the gall to send it to the greatest living musical theater genius on the planet. No, best keep that to himself.

"Is King writing anything lately?" someone asked.

Ethan Hancock shook his head. "Nothing I know of. The poor man is still recovering from *Black Hawk Down*. A genius, undoubtedly, but a lost talent."

That earned another classroom twitter – all these years later and the idea that King thought such an idea could be a hit still seemed amusing. But now that Ben had met King, despite his ill-treatment, wasn't it wrong to call King a lost-talent? Even *Black Hawk Down* had some beautiful music and brilliant lyrics. Clearly, there was some backstory – ill feelings or professional jealousy – between King and Ethan Hancock that Ben didn't know.

"A sad case, ladies and gentlemen," Ethan went on. "A cautionary tale. Now who's first up today? I believe we have a few more charm songs from *Lolita*?"

Ben had no desire to go first. But that was the trouble with collaboration. Before he knew it, untalented Drew had raised his hand.

"Good," Ethan said. "Thank you. Let's hear from Drew and Ben."

Ben felt himself rise to his feet.

"Go for it," Jen whispered.

Ben shuddered. This was one of those times he wished he could go home and cower under his old spinet piano. A charm song from *Lolita*? Most of the efforts from his classmates had been bad enough. But Ben knew that his and Drew's was a true misfire. Even so, Ben, the composer in this instance, sat at the piano, gathered himself, and then nervously played his mediocre introduction. Then Drew began to sing his altogether terrible lyrics.

Hey, Lolita!
So nice to meet a
Girl like you.

Hey, Lolita!
Pull up a seat a
My love is true.

Well, Ben thought as he played. At least they were true rhymes.

4

Three days later found Ben in the East Village with his roommate and college buddy, Harrison Billings. Both young men held cell phones, but not to check their email or make calls. Rather, they had been tasked by their new employer, *The Association for a Better City*, to photograph garbage in front of storefronts, said pictures to be used to punish consistent violators of litter laws.

"Check it out," Harrison said. "I got a good angle over here."

Ben sighed. What else could he do? A young actor, studying at the Village Playhouse, Harrison was a true artist; he even insisted on taking beautiful pictures of trash.

"Great," Ben said vaguely.

In truth, though he was happy to have another "money job," albeit a strange one, Ben still couldn't think about anything other than what had happened at the workshop.

"Oh, come on," Harrison said, trotting over to show Ben his photo, a gutter shot of an upside-down Starbucks cup and gnawed popsicle stick. "This is art."

Ben forced a smile. He had to admit that as pictures of garbage went, Harrison's were good.

"Nice work."

Harrison sighed. "You're thinking about it again, aren't you?"

"What?" Ben replied, though he knew perfectly well what his friend was talking about. After all, he hadn't been able to talk about anything else for the past three days. The day it had happened, he had kept Harrison up until two a.m., then woke Gretchen and continued venting until four.

"Let that go."

Ben nodded. "I know. But it's hard."

"So what if the teacher is difficult?"

"Difficult is one thing," Ben said. "If he had only been difficult, I might've survived."

It had been ugly. As Ben had predicted, his charm song from *Lolita* had not been well-received. After the horrific lyrics had been dissected and discarded, the class had turned its attention to the music. To Ben's surprise, the first comments had been nicer than expected. Tiffany Holt had called his melody "pleasant." Trying to throw in some moral support, Jen had called it "a good tune." No less than Steve Andrews had complimented a flourish of augmented chords. But then Ethan had lowered the boom.

"The music?" he had intoned. "As Stravinsky said about Handel, and I paraphrase, 'it's somewhat beautiful but oh so boring.'"

After taking in Ethan's sage opinion – and there was nothing he could do but sit there and take it – it had been all Ben could do to pour himself into a cab to his apartment, questioning his life decisions. Why the arts? Eleanor Crumb was a great editor but paid notoriously low advances. Couldn't he have been a kindergarten teacher? An accountant? Weren't plumbers well-paid? That Ben had gotten a new money-job photographing garbage the very next day hadn't done much to ease the pain.

"Okay," Harrison was saying now. "I get it, man. I do. But it's just one opinion about a dumb tune for a dumb assignment. I mean, a charm song? From *Lolita*? That's insanity!"

Ben laughed. What else could he do? Harrison was right. That's what made it more painful. He had been trashed for something he didn't even care about.

"Still sucks," he said.

"You don't even like this Ethan guy," Harrison said. "Wasn't he the guy that you told me Horatio King called a hack?"

Ben nodded. "Yep. But to be fair, that might be Horatio King's problem. I think his music is good. I liked *Stepping Out*."

Harrison waved a hand. "Whatever. He's probably jealous of you."

"Of me?"

"It's possible! Listen, I told you about what happened to me a week ago. In acting class? Remember?"

Of course, Ben remembered. Harrison had told him ten times.

"I know," Ben said. "Your teacher said, 'I don't believe a damn thing you're saying up there.'"

"Right," Harrison said. "I don't believe a damn thing. Not a single word. She thought I was faking it. And you know what? She was right. I was playing Stanley Kowalski like I was Elmer Fudd. So the next class I came back. I got in touch with my inner Yosemite Sam. I killed it. That's how it goes in this career. You're up then you're down then you're up again. Hang in there. Now who's the published author?"

Ben shrugged. He hated that his friend felt the need to pull out the ace card so quickly.

"I am, I guess," Ben said.

"You guess?" Harrison said. "You are and with the best kids' editor in the city, right?"

It was true.

"Yes, right."

It was then that Ben noticed it – the awning for *The Island*, New York's largest independent bookstore. Harrison acted fast, grabbing Ben's hand.

"Come on," he said.

"Where are we going?"

"You know where."

"Now?"

"Follow me."

"But…"

"Now!"

What else could Ben do? In truth, he was feeling that low. So he allowed his friend to pull him inside the large store, then up the stairs to the children's section.

"Where do they keep the middle-grade novels anyway?" Harrison asked.

"Actually," Ben murmured. "My book is still under New and Noteworthy."

Harrison's eyes lit up. "Ah, New and Noteworthy! Very good."

"Over there," Ben said.

In truth, he had been to the store over the past month to admire his book on the shelf before. And there it was again – right where it had been the other times Ben had looked – the gorgeous cover in rich purples and oranges, the roller-skating apple pies, all embellished by ornately designed letters that spelled, *The Worldwide Dessert Contest*. Then below in golden script, "By Ben Willis." It still took his breath away.

Harrison took the book off the shelf. "Look at it this. You did this, man. Have I written a book? No."

"True," Ben said. "But you have been on Broadway."

"Off Broadway," Harrison said. "In a ten-line part."

"Still, it's cool."

"This is cooler," Harrison said, shoving the book under his

friend's nose. "This is way cooler."

With the book still under his nose it was all Ben could do not to open it up and take a whiff of the pages. He might have, too, if not for a voice behind him.

"Can I help you guys find anything?"

Ben and Harrison spun around. Facing them was a young woman with short dark hair, and light blue eyes, wearing red lipstick. Her nose was on the flat side – in fact, Ben was reminded of a cartoon character who has been whacked by a frying pan – but flat nose or not, he liked the sum effect. Even so, he didn't want to be found out looking at his own book.

"No, no," he said. "We're good."

Which is when Harrison decided his friend needed an intervention beyond his career. Harrison – who had a serious boyfriend, a fellow acting student, Justin – had been telling Ben that he needed to talk to Gretchen less and find a "real girl." Meaning, one in the city, one that could last.

"We're better than good," Harrison said. "See this book? My buddy here wrote it."

The woman looked impressed. "Cool. I've seen the cover. *The Worldwide Dessert Contest*."

"Published by the best editor in the business," Harrison said. "Eleanor Crumb."

"Harrison," Ben said. He turned to the salesgirl. "Sorry. I guess I'm here checking in on my own work."

"Totally normal," the salesgirl said. She paused. "Actually…I have a YA novel out and I check on it all the time. I almost don't want people to buy it so I can look at it on the shelf."

Out of the corner of his eye, Ben could see his friend's face light up. "Ah, so you're a writer, too?" Harrison practically shouted it. "This is so cool."

"What's the name of your book?" Ben asked.

"*Cabin Four*," the girl said. "It's sort of a heartfelt girl-thing about a summer camp."

"Nice," Harrison said. "Ben loves summer camp, don't you, Ben? You went for what? Five summers?"

"Six," Ben murmured.

"Cool," the woman said. "Your book looks much funnier. Mine has a dead horse in it and a divorce." She smiled. "I basically pull on every heartstring."

Ben shrugged. "Well, mine has roller-skating apple pies. That's pretty sad."

The girl laughed. "Sorry. Dead animals beat skating pies – in terms of pathos, anyway."

"Whatever," Harrison said. "Ben and I love dead horse books. Let's see it."

"Really?"

"Yeah," Ben said, sincerely. "We'd love to."

It didn't take much convincing. The young woman turned on her heels and marched to the YA section, walked down the aisle past the "A's" all the way to the "R's."

"Here you go," she said.

Ben snapped back to the issue at hand: young adult literature.

There it was – the title *Cabin Four* with the picture of a girl and a stately brown horse in a pasture.

Then there was the name, in gentle cursive.

"Mo Ryan."

"That's me," the girl said. "And you're Ben Willis, I guess?"

Ben nodded. "Yep. And uh, this is Harrison, my roommate."

"This is sweet," Harrison said. "Tell you what, I'm going to browse in the drama section. Meet you out front in ten minutes, okay, Ben?"

Ben was about to object. Then he looked back at Mo. She was smiling – was it hopefully?

"Sure," he said to Harrison. "Ten minutes."

But then Ben heard it: the "bring" of a text.

"Go ahead," Mo said.

"No," Ben said. "I'm addicted but it can wait."

Mo seemed pleased. "Hey, listen. I get a break now anyway. Want to go to the café for a quick cup of coffee?"

But Ben had lied. He couldn't wait. He took a glance at his phone. Then he shuddered.

"CALL IMMEDIATELY! H. King."

"Who is it?" Mo asked.

Ben felt weak at the knees, stupefied. Why did Horatio King want him to call? Was Harrison or Gretchen pulling a prank? No, it was unlike them. Besides, the return number was one he didn't recognize.

"Sorry," Ben said. "I actually do have to get this."

5

"I'm gay, though of course you know that already," Horatio King said. It was a day later. Once again, Ben was following the great composer from his foyer to his living room. "But don't worry. I didn't invite you back to jump you. I've had my flings with young men – you've maybe heard about that, too – but those days are over."

King plopped down in his customary spot on the sofa. Sitting himself, Ben felt a wave of relief. Yes, over the phone, he had said he wanted to talk more about the "dessert project." But in truth, Ben had worried that Horatio King was looking for something more than a writing partner.

"Besides," King went on. "I'm eighty-five now. I can barely drive let alone have sex."

Ben laughed. "Understood."

"Don't be so quickly amused," King said. He reached into his pocket and swallowed a pill with a gulp of water. "You'll be my age before you know it. It goes by fast, young man. But in a way, it's a good thing. You won't always feel so desperate."

That got Ben's attention. "Desperate? Me?"

King raised his eyebrows. "Of course you."

Ben didn't know whether to be pissed off or laugh. Wasn't he seeing Mo, author of *Cabin Four* later that week? Hadn't he parlayed their quick in-store meeting into a date?

"What's that supposed to mean?" Ben said. "You don't know me."

King waved a hand. "I'm a writer, Mr. Willis. I know your type."

To most anyone else, Ben might have had the self-respect to say "fuck off" and leave. But to Horatio King? Ben sat still and took it. Besides, there was a part of him that was interested in what he was going to say. And he didn't have to wait long. Because just like that, King's cane was firmly planted on the floor and he was on his feet, pacing the room.

"You get women easily, that's my guess," King said.

"Not really," Ben said. "I mean, sometimes…occasionally."

King wrinkled his brow. "Occasionally, huh? Your problem isn't sex, it's love."

Ben sucked in a deep breath. Hadn't he been in love with Gretchen back in college? (He had told her once, anyway). Hadn't they just pledged to marry at forty-three and a half?

"I've been in love," Ben said.

King shot him a sideways glance, eyebrows raised. "Her name?"

"Gretchen."

"And are you still in love with this Gretchen?"

Ben shrugged. "Sort of."

King waved his cane. "Ah, ha! She probably wanted a commitment somewhere along the line, but you hesitated, am I right?"

He was right – senior year of college right after Ben had uttered his famous one-time "I love you" – but the hell if Ben was going to admit it.

"You didn't invite me back to analyze me, did you?"

King chuckled "Not analyze you, boy." Then he looked Ben square in the eye. "But I do like to know a thing or two about a person before I collaborate."

Ben blinked. Had he heard that correctly?

"You know, Bernard Tannenbaum?" King went on. "My book-writer for *Black Hawk Down*?"

"I know of him."

"Hooked on painkillers," King exclaimed. "And my book-writer for *Moses and Me*? She went after her parakeet with an axe. The bird was lucky to get away. I damn near got scalped saving it."

"Christ," Ben said.

"And we all know what Richard Rodgers had to do to take care of Larry Hart," King went on, warming to his subject. "The poor man was a genius, of course, but Rodgers had to sometimes search up and down the city, then sober him up to get him to write a lyric. A collaboration is like a marriage, you know. If I'm to work with you, I need to know if I'm going to find you puking your guts out at a "rave" or whatever it is that your generation calls a party. I need to know if you'll be unable to work one day because you're home slobbering in your blanket over some floozy. I'm eighty-five, going on ninety-one. Most musicals take five to ten years to get to Broadway. I don't want to be dead or, worse, drooling in a cup at our opening. We'll need to work extremely fast and with concentration. Do you understand?"

Ben was flabbergasted. Yes, he had been hopeful that King wanted to talk further about his book, but this was entirely unexpected.

"So wait," he said, sitting forward. His heart was thumping like it was going to bunny-hop out of his chest. "You want to collaborate? On a musical?"

"No," King said. "On a dog-walking business. Of course, a musical! Why in fuck's name do you think I texted?"

"But you hate my book," Ben said. "You made fun of it."

"Just a little."

"You threw a Tony at my head."

"I didn't hit you, did I?"

Ben shook his head.

"So what's the problem? No harm done."

"But you hate my book. You called it a cookbook."

"Shut up about that, already," King said. "Do I look senile? Yes, I'm slightly withered and I walk with a cane, but last I checked I can remember what happened less than a week ago." King frowned, looking Ben up and down. "Maybe this was a mistake."

"No, no. I'm just confused. What changed your mind?"

King shrugged. For a spilt second, Ben thought he looked a bit embarrassed. Then he sat down, again across from him.

"Honestly?" he said.

"Of course. Yes."

"I read the damned thing."

Ben's eyes went wide. "You hadn't even read any of it before?"

"Do you know how many letters and requests I get?" King said. "I can't read every ridiculous thing some young punk with a pretty face sends me."

"Then what made you read mine?"

"Well," King said. "The truth is I was sitting right here, bored, not sure what to do when Juniper trotted over. To my surprise, the dog was holding your book in his wet jaws."

"He was?"

King nodded. "So you have this furry animal to thank, I guess," giving Juniper a rough scratch. "He dropped the book in my lap like it was a damned bone. What else could I do? From such gestures, empires are built. I read a page. It was good. I read another. Then another after that. Two and a half hours passed, and I was done. Then I looked at some of the lyrics you sent along." King leaned forward now, eyes glistening. "My boy, why didn't you tell me that you were talented?"

Ben blinked. How could he answer such an absurd question? "Well, I…"

"Shut up, don't answer that. It was my mistake. I thought a straight, decent-looking boy couldn't be good. But I guess this Eleanor Crumb knows what she's doing. Your book is charming. Funny. It made me do something I haven't done much of lately – laugh." King chuckled. "Changing desserts! Roller-skating apple pies. Odd but ingenious!"

Ben was overcome. Had Horatio King just called something of his "ingenious?"

"So you like it?"

"What, are you deaf? I just said I did."

Ben was stunned. "Thanks," he stammered. "So wait?" He still couldn't believe it. "You really want to do this?"

"Truthfully, I'm as surprised as you." King looked Ben in the eye. "But everything I get sent is so damned depressing! I figure fifteen or so years is enough time to sulk over a flop, don't you? I'm a writer, after all – a damn good one – and writers write. Your story touched something in me. Something about the hero's unrelenting urge to win this stupid contest spoke to me. It's a metaphor for us all, isn't it? Winning the dessert contest of life?" He picked up the book. "There's hope in these pages." He continued, almost shyly. "I actually took the time to dash off some music to your opening love song. The one Applefeller sings to his world's largest apple pancake."

"You did?" Ben couldn't believe it. He couldn't wait to tell Gretchen. Horatio King had written music to one of his lyrics!

But then he remembered. "Wait, I already wrote music to that one."

King raised a single eyebrow. "Your music?"

"Yeah…"

Ben could see where this was going.

"Let's be real here, boy," King said. "Mine'll be better."

Ben began to object but stopped himself. After all, most assuredly, King was right.

"Do you want to hear it or not?" the old man said, impatiently.

Ben nodded. "Yes, yes, very much."

With that, King pointed to an adjoining room.

"Come then."

Ben followed the shambling man into a medium-sized study whose main piece of furniture was a grand piano covered with neatly stacked piles of printed scores, all by King himself. Along with *Lear* and *Black Hawk Down* were the scores to *Jumpers*, *Billy Budd*, *Corporate Law*, *Moses and Me,* and *Evergreen* – all King hits. The walls were covered with photos of King with famous theater luminaries, a mayor or two, and a governor. Aside from that, there was a well-worn sofa and an easy chair. It was a small space, but home of the creation of some of the world's greatest theater in the last generation.

"All right," King said, shuffling through a pile of music on the bench. "Where did I put it? I wrote out a lead sheet."

A few pieces of paper fell to the floor. As the old man stooped to pick them up, Ben rushed over to help then set the papers back on the music stand.

"Ah, here it is."

Just as the great man was sitting down, Juniper jumped onto the piano bench.

"Fuck off," King said, nudging the dog to the floor with his butt. "This is work time."

He played a chord. Ben didn't have the ear of Steve Andrews, but he recognized a Major Seventh when he heard it. Then just like that, a dream came true: Horatio King raised his gravelly, old-man voice and sang his tune to the lyric Ben had written, a love song sung by John Applefeller to the world's largest apple pancake.

Golden Brown.
Fluffy, too.
My apple pancake.
Samantha, girl
If you only knew
The pancake I've made.
Ten feet wide and three feet thick,
So fluffy you could die.
It's the golden-brown apple of my eye.

How I worked
All year through
On my apple pancake.
But it was time, I'm telling you,
That I never would trade.
Some men have a family they put nothing else above.
I've a golden-brown pancake to love!

Apple pancake, can't you see?
You'll be the dessert to make a man of me.
Apple pancake, golden as the moon.
When the judges taste you,
I'll win the Silver Spoon.

And then they'll know, then they'll see,
The pancake
I can bake.
But all the world will honor me,
The top of the grade.
I'll show them what dessert can be,
A pancake large and apple-y,
Mixed the with love, baked with joy,
Stuffed with hope and heart,
It's a golden-brown work of art.

And by the way, please don't change!

"So?" King asked when he was done. "Have I lost it?"

To Ben's surprise, the old man was nervous.

"It's beautiful," Ben said.

Indeed, it had been – a rush of melody and harmony that had built to a surprising climax, making for a touching, unusual love song. King smiled.

"Better than yours?"

Ben laughed. "Much."

With that, King nodded, satisfied. Then he stood and slid a blank piece of paper and a pen across the top of the piano.

"What's this for?" Ben asked.

"In your first song," King began. "The Man with the Changing Desserts." You have some nice lines – you're talented enough to write the lyrics for this show, I think, and I'm not as young as I used to be. But your words need massaging. So sit. I'll give you notes, you revise. Then I'll get after the tune."

Ben hesitated. Did King expect him to get to work right away?

"Tick, tock, Mr. Willis! Last I looked, I'm still eighty-five."

6

The following week, Ben all but lived at Horatio King's apartment, only returning home to shave, shower, and sleep. The first few days were given over to going through the book chapter by chapter, picking appropriate scenes to dramatize. Working quickly but thoroughly, the collaborators laser-focused on the plot, adjusting the book to fit the musical. The villain Sylvester Sweet was given a sister, Dentina, to fall in love with Applefeller. German dessert chef Princess Irma Frostina was given a comic fixation with Head Judge Nathaniel Barkle's caramel apple. The three assistant judges—Brewster McLaughlin, the sugar specialist; Hamilton Crusthardy, the cake expert; and George Saucery, the ice cream analyst—were given love interests, then made single again when Ben and King realized it would make for too large a cast.

"These men will be judges, plain and simple," King said. "Not lovers."

As the pair turned their attention to the opening number, "The Man with the Changing Desserts," Ben experienced King's famous work ethic firsthand. Again and again, he had Ben discard or rewrite a lyric. Again and again, he shook his head and muttered "excrement" or "no, no, never!" over a perfectly fine phrase of music. And the work didn't end when Ben left the apartment. At home, with friends, or even on the rounds photographing garbage, Ben soon got used to receiving texts from the great master.

Some were strictly informative:

"Working tonight on the dance music..."

Some were contemplative:

"Sometimes I think I'm better than Rodgers and Gershwin combined. Your thoughts?"

Some were combative:

"Your latest lyric is a disgrace. Dessert and Quirk do not rhyme! Call me!"

Luckily, King wasn't all ruthless criticism. Though compliments were rare, they were sincere and enthusiastic.

"Hell, yes!" King shouted one afternoon over a line that pleased him–so loudly that Juniper woke with a loud yap. "That's not bad."

By the end of a week, the collaborators had their opening— a musical scene that dramatized Applefeller's strange history with changing desserts set to a sprightly, chromatic tune that only King could have written. Then the pair turned to other musical possibilities.

"*Hmmm,*" King said. It was early afternoon, and the collaborators had just finished lunching on a delivery of Thai food. They were in the study, both lounging on the couch. "We need a big song for the Ragoon at the end of Act One."

"Right," Ben said.

"Something where the Ragoon decides to come back to the real world from Iambia and take on Sylvester Sweet," King went on.

"Something stirring," Ben said.

King nodded. "An anthem."

With that, the old man took a final bite of curry, threw his paper plate in the trash, then stepped over a sleeping Juniper to the piano. Ben couldn't help but notice that the entire endeavor left him slightly winded – walking across the room from a standing start was almost more than he could handle.

"Something like this," King said, lowering himself to the piano bench. He began to play, bringing to life a stirring march. As had happened again and again, Ben experienced a moment of standing outside himself, watching, amazed. Was he really writing with the great King? Rumors that his talent had slipped were notably incorrect, clearly mired in ignorance and jealousy. The music he was improvising was thrilling and harmonically lush.

"I love it," Ben said. "But what should the lyric be?"

King smiled, playing an arpeggio. "That's your problem, kid. I'm just writing the music for this show. But something about the glory of dessert, I would think."

With that, King improvised some more, each new motif inspired by what he played a moment before, creating a cascade of sound that fed and built off of itself.

"Make it big," King said. "Make it funny."

Ben took a moment to drink in the gorgeous harmonies filling the room. Then he scribbled a line on his notepad.

"How's this?" he said, sliding it nervously toward the old man.

Some people bake a dessert and ask why?
Why does this taste make me shiver and sigh?

King grunted with appreciation and adjusted his improvisation to fit the words. Within seconds, he was he barking out a tune in a gravelly baritone.

"That'll work," King said. "But what next?"

Which is when Ben had an inspiration. A student of history,

he had always admired the Kennedys. Was it luck or fate that his first couplet echoed one of Robert Kennedy's most well-known speeches? Whatever the reason, Ben hurriedly wrote another line. Then he crossed it out and wrote another, and another after that.

"You look energized," King said, still playing.

"I am," Ben said.

He crossed out what he had written again and wrote a final couplet. This one he liked.

"Here," he said. "You play, I'll sing."

King did as he was told. Holding his scrap paper with trembling fingers, Ben raised his undistinguished voice, doing his best to fit the spirit of King's music.

Some people bake a dessert and ask why?
Why does this taste make me shiver and sigh?
But I think of tastes that could sure hit the spot.
That have not yet been baked and wonder 'why not?'

King burst out laughing.

"My, boy, brilliant!"

Ben was practically giddy. Had Horatio King just called something he had written: "Brilliant?" He almost couldn't believe his ears.

"Thanks."

"Don't get cocky," King growled. "You aren't finished. Write the next lines. Come on then."

Ben looked at the paper. In his experience, writer's block came when what he was trying to write was no good. When inspired, he wrote quickly. And now he had hit the mother lode. In a flash, he jotted down the next quatrain.

Why not bake a pie that can speak in Chinese?
Or a pie that says "bless you" whenever you sneeze?
Why not bake a pie you can fly in the air like a kite?
Or a pie to take dancing on Saturday night?

Ben laid it on the keyboard. King squinted and laughed, but then scowled.

"What?" Ben said. "You don't like it?"

"'In the air' is redundant," King said. "Where else do you fly a fucking kite?"

Ben crossed out the offending words.

"Anything else?" Ben asked.

"Yes," King scowled. "A final verse. Close this baby with a bang."

Ben sat back on the sofa. What would be the best way to finish the song? He was drawing a blank. Luckily, King wasn't.

"You've used one Kennedy," he called, still working on the bridge, or B section, of the song. "Why not another for the last verse?"

Ben saw it in a flash. President Kennedy's famous inaugural address!

"Got you," Ben said. "Give me a second."

He stood and paced. He wrote a line. He crossed it out. He wrote another. Then he ran to his laptop and clicked on *rhymezone.com*. He checked rhymes for "desserts" and then took a new sheet of paper. All the while, King was industriously playing at the piano. His patience was soon rewarded. This time, the first line Ben wrote was a keeper. In two more minutes, he was done.

"Got it," he said.

"Show me!"

Ben laid it his paper out on the piano.

For I live by a creed, noble and true.
Don't ask what dessert can do for you.
Instead, you must bake, bake til it hurts.
And ask yourself what you can do for desserts!

"Yes, yes," King said. "Quite right, boy. Quite right!"
King stopped, and scribbled some notes on a piece of music manuscript. Then he played another flourish of chords and wrote more notes. Then he hummed to himself, played a final harmony, and finished notating.
"Ready to hear the whole thing?" he said,
Ben nodded. King sang the completed song.

Some people bake a dessert and ask why?
Why does this taste make me shiver and sigh?
But I think of tastes that could sure hit the spot
That have not yet been baked and wonder, "Why not?"

Why not bake a pie that can speak in Chinese?
Or a pie that will bless you whenever you sneeze?
Why not bake a pie you can fly like a kite?
Or a pie to take dancing on Saturday night!

For I live by a dream, noble and true.
Don't ask what desserts can do for you.
Instead, you must bake. Bake til it hurts.
And ask yourself what you can do for desserts!

It was beautiful, lush music – dramatic music that expertly

explicated the Ragoon's most deeply held dessert beliefs, giving him motivation to return back to civilization to take on Sylvester Sweet. Proud of the lyric, Ben was eager to show it off.

"I'll play it for the workshop tomorrow," he said.

King had other ideas. The old man was on his feet like he had been branded.

"No, no, no," he said, waving a finger. "You will not play this beautiful song for anyone, not yet – especially not in that grotesquerie of a workshop."

Ben blinked. Yes, he knew King hated AMI, but wasn't this extreme?

"I have to present a new song every few weeks. It's the rule."

"Find a trunk tune."

"A trunk tune?" Ben said. "I'm only twenty-five."

"Some trash you wrote in college then," King said. "News of our collaboration is premature."

"Is it?" Ben squeaked. He realized his voice was shaking, his breath short. He had a horrible thought. Was King thinking about backing out? Had Ben been wrong to tell anyone at all? "I've already mentioned it to some friends."

King nodded. "Your *BFFs*, of course. And that's fine. I'm not a total monster. But let's make sure the work is good enough before we shout it from the rooftops. Because if we announce our show now or play a song in the AMI workshop everyone will want to see the whole damned thing. I still am Horatio King, right? Can't you just hear the questions? 'Why the hell are you writing a musical about a dessert contest?' they'll ask. 'He's writing a musical where one of the main characters has a fucking caramel apple stuck to his face.' Trust me on this. It'll be a blood sport. They'll crucify us! When we're finished and we know it's good, we'll have a reading. Word will get out soon enough then we'll hope for the best."

And so the next afternoon, at AMI, Ben didn't offer to play a new song for the class. He also bit his tongue when Ethan Hancock made another crack about King, referring to *Black Hawk Down* as "harmonically stagnant." And when Hancock asked Ben if he had anything to present, Ben answered with a white lie.

"I've been spending the last week or so working on another children's novel."

Ethan raised an eyebrow. Of the few people in the class who had read *The Worldwide Dessert Contest*, he wasn't one of them.

"More kiddie porn?" he said.

Ben let the crack pass. "Something like that."

"May I ask what about?"

Ben had no idea. In truth, he had been so busy working with King that he hadn't thought about it. He found himself stammering.

"What?" Ethan asked. "You don't know the subject of your own book?"

"Sure I do," Ben blurted. "It's about...a polar bear."

Just like that, Ben had his new idea – or at least a main character. To his relief, smiles of approval filled the room.

"Cool," Steve Andrews said. "I like polar bears."

"I'll second that," Tiffany Holt said. "I assume this bear talks?"

"Sure," Ben said, improvising. "It's a kids' novel."

"What does the bear do?" Jen asked. "Find a cure for global warming?"

"Bring peace to the Mid-East?"

"Fix the Electoral College?"

All valid, if outlandish, ideas. But Ben suddenly had another.

"I was thinking that the bear would write a musical," he said. Then he smiled. "With Horatio King."

Laughter filled the room, none louder than from Ethan Hancock.

"Ha!" he said with a snort. "That might be just what King needs to get the engines re-started. A children's musical!"

Ben smiled but bit his tongue.

A children's musical. Yes, indeed.

7

"So who's Gretchen?"

A simple question, but one that had Ben instantly back on his heels.

"Gretchen?" he asked.

He and Mo were seated by the window of a small Italian Restaurant on Second Avenue.

"*Hmm, hmm*," Mo said. "I'm working on my second glass of wine and it's the third time you've mentioned her. She seems significant."

Ben felt himself fighting back a blush. Had he been found out that quickly?

"She's just an old friend."

"Friend?"

"Okay, girlfriend," Ben said. "From college." Then he smiled. Why not come clean? "But we just made a vow to marry at forty-three and a half if we're still single."

To Ben's relief, Mo laughed.

"Oh, cool. Do you have one of those? I have one of those."

"A guy from college?"

"No, a girl."

"A girl? Ah."

"That's cool, isn't it?"

Ben nodded, ever the liberated man. "Of course. Who's the lady?"

"My best friend, Brynn. But our age is forty."

Mo took a final bite of her pasta. "How'd you settle on forty-three and a half?"

Ben laughed. "Pretty random. Gretchen thought that would still give her time to have a kid."

Mo nodded. "Makes sense."

She took another sip of wine as Ben watched. Harrison's instincts had been right. Mo was certainly cute, squashed nose and all. Better, they had more in common than he had imagined. Both were from New York (Manhattan) and had suffered the charmed ignominy of elite private schools. Both liked the Mets and the Natural History Museum. On top of that, Mo was cued in enough to have been appropriately awed by Ben's good fortune with Horatio King. In preparation for the date, they had even read each other's books. Toward the end of the meal, they doled out appropriate praise.

"Yours was hilarious," Mo said. "I loved it when the Ragoon's apple pies spoke in Swahili."

Ben smiled. He was especially proud of that.

"I liked yours, too," he said. "A lot."

He wasn't lying. He had found Mo's story amusing and touching without being sentimental.

"Especially the part where the horse dies, right?"

"How'd you know? To be honest, I cried. Well, a tear or two anyway."

"Well, that was the point."

"Are you thinking of another?" Ben asked.

"A sequel?" she said. "I sort of killed off the horse."

Ben smiled. "Not a sequel to this one. Another book? A new idea?"

"For real?" Mo replied. "I have an idea about a dystopia set in Botswana."

"Okay," Ben said slowly, not sure if it was a joke. "Botswana, huh? Sounds workable." Then he paused. Should he risk it? "If you need a reader, I'd be happy to look at it."

To Ben's relief, Mo seemed pleased. "I could use a reader or two. I actually got a Brody scholarship to work on it."

"A Brody Scholarship…?"

"They send you to London to write for six months."

Ben was impressed, but also surprised to find that he felt disappointed. "London, wow. That's a long way away."

"Just a plane ride," Mo said. "Anyway, if you'd like to read what I have when I'm ready that'd be great. But what about you? Do you have another idea?"

Ben shrugged. "Well, I don't know if I should be admitting such personal information but I just announced to my songwriting class that I was going to write a book about a polar bear."

"Cool. I love talking animal stories. *Charlotte's Web*, right?"

"Right."

"So what about this bear? What will it do?"

Ben laughed. "That's the problem. I don't know. I just know that he talks."

"Do you know his name?"

Ben shrugged. "I don't know. Whitney?"

Mo raised her glass. "I like it. Okay, here's to Whitney the talking polar bear."

Ben clinked his glass. "Yes, to Whitney! And African dystopias."

"Nice," Mo said.

They each drank.

"To tell the truth," Ben said, lowering his glass. "Gretchen says I should write a kids' book about the Tet Offensive."

"Ah, ha!" Mo said with a laugh. "Gretchen again! Four times!"

"I told you," Ben said. "We're just friends."

"Until you're forty-three and a half anyway."

"Right," Ben said.

Mo leaned closer.

"What?" Ben asked.

"Nothing…I guess that gives us some time then?"

With that observation, she reached across the table and took Ben's hand.

"Yeah," Ben said. He gave her hand a gentle squeeze, admiring her turquoise fingernails. "I guess it does."

After dinner, thoroughly drunk, Ben and Mo walked arm and arm down Second Avenue, on their way to Ben's apartment.

"It's a little bit messy," Ben said.

"I can deal with messy."

"It's a one-bedroom and I sleep in the living room on a Murphy bed."

Mo pinched his side. "You do realize this is only our first date. We may not get as far as pulling out the bed."

"Oh, I know," Ben said. "I just wanted to give you the lay of the land."

"Got it," Mo said, her arm back around his waist. "A roommate and a Murphy bed. Anything else? A shrine to your book, I suppose?"

"Oh, yes. Of course. In neon. I hope it's okay but you have to kiss a copy of *The Worldwide Dessert Contest* before entering the room."

"I wouldn't expect anything different. I'll lick the chapter where the apple pies finally fly."

Ben laughed. "That would be an honor. Get ready because we're almost there."

"Okay, then. Anything else I should know?"

Ben thought a moment. "Well," he said. "I guess I should mention the rat corral."

Mo stopped short.

"A rat *what*?"

"Yeah," Ben said. "We had a little problem with vermin."

Mo laughed uneasily. "A little problem? Is there such a thing?"

"Not really," Ben said. "We live on the first floor. Turns out the contractor didn't fully block the wall behind the sink."

"So rats came up from the basement?" Mo asked.

Ben nodded. "Exactly. But don't worry, we finally got it fixed. The holes were blocked and the rats went away."

"Rats, not mice?"

Ben shook, shivering himself at the memory. "Rats. Sad to say."

Mo shivered. "Gross. So what was the rat corral?"

"Before we had the wall fixed, we built a corral of cinder blocks around the kitchen. So if a rat appeared it couldn't get into the rest of the apartment."

"Did it work?"

Ben nodded. "Actually, yes. Though it got tiring having to climb over a three-foot gate of cinder blocks every time we wanted to get to the fridge."

"I take it the corral has been deconstructed?"

"In full," Ben said. "You can see for yourself."

He pointed up a stone staircase to a brownstone.

"*Hmmm*," Mo said. "Suddenly, I don't feel so eager to go inside."

"No, no," Ben said. Had the talk of rats taken his policy of "honesty at all costs" a step too far? "It's okay. The rats are gone."

Mo looked up the steps and then back at Ben. "You promise?"

Ben moved closer. "Yeah. Come on."

Suddenly, Mo kissed Ben full on the mouth.

"Remember," she said. "First date. No Murphy Bed."

Ben had thought Harrison was going to be out already, spending the night at Justin's. Instead, the timing was off. As he and Mo pushed into the apartment, Harrison was emerging from the shower in a towel.

"Alas, Poor Yorick!" he intoned. "I knew him, Horatio: a fellow of infinite jest, of most excellent fancy: he hath borne me on his back a thousand times;"

"You didn't tell me you lived with Hamlet," Mo whispered.

"Nope," Ben said. "Just an actor."

Harrison stopped short, finally breaking character.

"Worry not. There was a slight delay because Justin has to see a friend in a one-person show downtown. But I'll vacate the premises soon."

"What's it about?" Mo asked. "The show, I mean?"

Harrison shrugged. "Not sure. But I think his friend plays a giant amoeba."

"An amoeba? Sounds very Off Broadway."

"Doesn't it?" Harrison said. "I'm going to run some lines in my room for a while. Have fun."

With that, he slipped into his room, letting his towel fall to the floor as he shut the door.

"Not bad," Mo said. "I got a little bit of Shakespeare and got to see your roommate's butt."

"Don't worry," Ben said. "He'll leave us alone."

Mo nodded, seemingly unconcerned.

"Ah ha," she said, turning her attention to the kitchen. "The site of the famous rat corral."

"That's right," Ben said.

He came up from behind and put his arms around her waist. Mo leaned back into him.

"So these rats," Mo asked. "Were they big?"

"As big as gophers."

"That's reassuring."

"Actually, more like dogs."

"Wow. Standard poodles?"

"Dobermann's."

Mo laughed. "Rats the size of Dobermann's, huh?"

Ben knew what was happening: the time-honored ritual, a round of "stupid talk" before kissing.

"Yep. We once heard two of them having a fight."

"A fight?"

"Yep. Harrison found one of them dead in the kitchen in the morning. To his credit, he picked the thing up by its tail and threw it out."

"By the tail?" Mo asked. "A rat as big as a Dobermann?"

"Harrison's stronger than he looks."

Mo turned around. Ben held her close.

"You really know how to charm a girl."

"I try."

They kissed and moved quickly to the couch. Yes, Mo had warned him not to expect much. On the other hand, she was kissing him like an appearance by the Murphy Bed was a foregone conclusion.

"You feel good," she whispered.

"You, too."

Mo laughed. "Better than Gretchen?

"Ask me when I'm forty-three and a half."

Ben ran his tongue along Mo's neck.

"*Hmmm*, nice," Mo said.

"I was hoping you'd think that."

With that, he settled her on the couch. They lay down, wrapped in each other's arms. Mo returned the favor, licking Ben's neck. Which is when he heard a light bring pierce the silence. A text. Mo looked over her shoulder. Ben's phone was sitting a foot away on the piano bench.

"Ignore it," Ben said.

Mo laughed.

"It's him, right?"

"Him?"

"Horatio King."

Ben had mentioned his proclivity for inopportune texts.

"Ignore it," Ben said. "Doesn't matter."

He kissed Mo again.

The text bringed again.

Mo pulled away.

"Answer it," she said, sitting up. "This is getting a little hot and heavy for me anyway."

Ben was tempted to point out that "hot and heavy" was his goal. Instead, he quickly adjusted his pants and reached for his phone. Mo was right – it was pure Horatio King.

We need a song for the goddamned judge about how the goddamned caramel apple got stuck to his face. Thoughts?

Mo read the text over Ben's shoulder.

"Delicate guy, huh?"

"Totally," Ben said. "I think he's uttered maybe two sentences since we've met without cursing."

"Well, sounds important," Mo said. "You'd better answer."

"No, it can wait."

Ben kissed her again. Mo pushed him back.

"Go ahead. He's old, right? Don't want him stroking out before you finish the show."

"True," Ben said.

"Type. I'll wait."

So Ben did.

I'll work on it tomorrow and get you a lyric.

He pressed send, then slid back to Mo, took her in his arms, and kissed her again, making up for lost time, moving back to her neck and allowing his right hand to slide underneath the back of her shirt, feeling skin.

"You feel awfully nice," he whispered.

"You, too. Your hand is under my shirt."

"Oh, is it? I wasn't aware."

He unbuttoned her top button, half expecting her to make him stop. She didn't. In fact, she took care of the second button.

"My shirt seems to be falling off," she murmured.

"I'm noticing," Ben said.

As he was reaching for button three, he heard the bring – again! Again, Mo pulled back.

"Better get that."

"Nope," Ben said.

He kissed her again and unbuttoned the third button. The shirt slipped off. Ben took his off, too. Then to his surprise, Mo reached for the cord to the Murphy Bed and pulled it down.

"You sure?" Ben asked.

Mo nodded. "Don't ruin the moment."

Ben dived on and Mo followed, getting on top.

Bring!

"Oh, Christ," Mo said. "The poor man."

Ben sighed. He was thrilled to be collaborating with the great King. On the other hand, there were limits.

"I'm turning it off. The phone, I mean."

Mo handed it to him but read the message.

Call me post haste! I need to play you the theme from Roller Skating Pies. Are you free or with the floozy?

Ben was mortified.

"Oh, God. I've never called you a floozy."

Mo didn't seem concerned. "Of course, you didn't."

"That's just how he is," Ben said.

"So what are you going to answer?" Mo asked.

"This," Ben said.

He took his phone.

She's not a floozy. Happy to talk apple desserts in the AM.

With that, he turned off the phone.

"There, he's gone."

"Wow," Mo said. "Did you just sort of hang up on an eight-time Tony winner?"

Ben nodded. "I did."

Mo laughed. "You must really want to get laid."

Ben could feel himself blush. "I have my priorities."

As if on cue, clothes came off. In seconds, Mo was under the covers, naked in Ben's arms. Ben reached for a rubber from his night table.

"I like a boy who's prepared," Mo whispered.

It was as Ben was reaching under the covers to slide on the rubber that he heard it – a squeak by the kitchen. At first, he thought it was another text. Then he thought it was the refrigerator. But quickly, he realized. In truth, he hadn't been completely honest with Mo. Yes, the rats were gone…mostly. An occasional critter – not as big as a Doberman but large enough – was known to show himself and then scamper away. While Ben and Harrison had vowed to call back the exterminator, their once again busy schedules coupled with heavy doses of inertia had delayed it. Sadly, this particular rodent wasn't content to mosey through the kitchen and then return to its hole in the wall. Instead, it wandered out to the living room.

As Mo got on top of Ben, he noticed a shadow on the wall. They both heard the squeak – again – and loudly. Then, to Ben's dismay, Mo was suddenly standing on the bed, naked, pointing wildly. But not at a rat at all.

"Raccoon!" she cried.

Ben gasped.

"It must've come over from the park!"

The animal was ambling closer.

"Do something!" Mo said.

Like any New Yorker, Ben had killed cockroaches and waterbugs. He had even given chase to his share of mice. A pigeon had once gotten loose in his family's living room. But a raccoon? In his apartment? While he was naked…and erect? That was more than even the most seasoned New Yorker could be expected to contend with.

"Well?" Mo said.

Luckily, Ben had a roommate who had just finished basic theater fight training. In a flash, Harrison was out of his room, bearing a broom. Still, in character from earlier in the night, he was swinging for blood.

"Begone, foul beast!"

The battle was epic but brief. With several quick parries, Harrison had the raccoon back in the kitchen where it rose to its haunches, bared its teeth, then scurried under the stove, disappearing into the bowels of the basement. Job done, Harrison returned to his room, calling, "Better finally call that exterminator. Next thing you know it'll be lemurs!" As his door slammed, Ben looked at Mo. To his horror, she was rifling for her underwear.

"Wait," Ben said. "He's gone now."

"Sorry, Ben. You're a nice guy." She was putting on her bra. "I can deal with Gretchen and your roommate's butt and with texts from Horatio King. I even could've dealt with a medium-sized rat – I'm used to them. But I draw the line at raccoons."

"We can go to your place," Ben said.

"I live in Queens by Citi Field."

"Perfect," Ben said. "We both like the Mets."

"Listen, Ben," Mo said with a not unsympathetic smile. "This was going a bit fast anyway. Tell you what? Clean up your apartment, block up those holes for good, and give me a holler, okay? I'm in town for another month."

What could Ben do, except clutch the blanket and steel himself for what was bound to be a horrific case of blue balls? Slipping on his underwear, he hobbled to the door and gave Mo a kiss.

"Well, I had fun, anyway," he said.

Mo smiled. "Call me."

"I will," Ben said. "But what am I going to do the rest of the night?"

A last-ditch attempt. Would she change her mind and stay? No. Instead, Mo gave him another kiss, this one with the feel of finality.

"From what I understand, there's a head judge with a caramel apple stuck to his face. He needs a song."

8

That weekend, Ben put his romantic woes on hold and worked diligently on a confessional song in which Head Judge Nathaniel Barkle related the tragic history of his caramel apple. Early Sunday evening, Ben sent the finished lyric to Horatio King.

BARKLE:
Once I led a happy life, each dessert-filled year.
Knew what pie that Shakespeare ate
Before he wrote King Lear.

(aside) Blueberry mango with whipped cream. It's fully documented in my treatise: "Elizabethan Desserts – part nine, opus three."

But then one day ten years ago!
Terrible! Tragic! Embarrassment! Torture! Humiliation!

In short, dessert disaster!

The breeze was blowing west.
The sky was gray.
And a caramel apple was sitting on a tray.
Sitting on a tray.

I picked the apple up.
With judgely grace.
But the caramel apple brushed against my face.
Brushed against my face.

First, I laughed, then gave the fruit a little nudge.
Then I yanked it hard, but still, it would not move.
Then everybody pulled, but no matter how they pulled,
It wouldn't budge!
A doctor, later, said: "It's sad but true.
There's absolutely nothing I can do.
The caramel has turned into
The world's most powerful glue!"

Oh, once I was a man.
Now I'm a disgrace!
With a caramel apple stuck upon my face.
Stuck upon my face! My face!

Finished, Ben went out with Harrison and Justin to a local bar for dinner, then home to catch up on some Netflix to complete an altogether uneventful evening. The next morning, however, Monday, the excitement came in a tidal wave, the news delivered by Ben's mother by way of an early morning phone call.

"Hey," Ben answered, groggily.

"Benjamin!"

No one else called him by his full name. And then, only when very excited.

"Hey, mom." Ben yawned. "What's up?"

In the way of all mothers, she got right to the point.

"Have you seen it yet?"

"Seen what?"

"Today's paper."

She meant the *Times*, of course.

"No," Ben said then stated the obvious. "You woke me."

No apology forthcoming.

"Go out and buy it."

"I read it online."

"Log on now...I'll wait."

"Mom...what's going on?"

Had someone died?

"I'll wait."

Ben stumbled out of bed to his small desk, opened his laptop, and logged on.

"The New York Times," his mom said.

"I know, mom. You said."

"Are you there yet?"

"No...Okay, now I am."

Ben took a seat.

"Good. Go to the theater section."

Ben's heart jumped. Had another new show been reviewed? His mother had been known to call to tout other people's success, an altogether irritating habit. But not this time. Ben's eye fixed on a headline so surprising, it took a long moment to fully comprehend.

MUSICAL ICON KING WORKING ON NEW SHOW
WITH FIRST-TIMER WILLIS

Ben gasped.

"I thought you said he didn't want to announce it yet," his mother said.

"That's what he said."

"Did he change his mind then?"

"I don't know. Or someone leaked it."

"Not me," his mother said. "Mum's been the word. Read the article. It seemed accurate to me, but what do I know?"

Ben moved the mouse to the headline and clicked. Opening before him was a picture of King from the time of *Black Hawk Down*, thirteen years earlier, beard a little less white and shaggy. To Ben's surprise, a few inches down the page was his headshot, the author's picture from *The Worldwide Dessert Contest*, an image of him sitting at a dining room table in front of a giant chocolate cake.

"My God," Ben said. "They pulled the picture from the book jacket. Probably from my website."

"Very handsome," his mother said. "Read it out loud."

"Out loud?" Ben asked. "Haven't you read it already?"

"Ten times. I want to hear it again."

What else could a son do? He cleared his throat and jumped in.

Musical Theater icon and winner of eight Tony Awards, Horatio King, contacted the Times yesterday afternoon to say that he is back at work after a near fifteen-year hiatus. 'I'm collaborating with a young writer named Ben Willis, musicalizing his novel, The Worldwide Dessert Contest,' King said. 'It's a musical comedy in the best old-fashioned sense of the term. Ben Willis's modern-day take on the human condition gives this children's piece an adult patina that makes for a scathing commentary on modern-day America.' King hopes the show will be on Broadway within a year or 'before I'm confined to a nursing home – whichever comes first.'

According to King, Willis is a talented young lyricist. The Worldwide Dessert Contest received starred reviews in both Booklist and Publisher's Weekly and was edited by the famous Eleanor Crumb.

Ben lowered the screen.

"My, God," Ben said. "He really did it. He changed his mind!"

The next hour was a flurry of phone calls, emails, and texts – friends from high school, college, summer camp, and even one from nursery school got in touch. None were more surprised than his fellow members of the AMI workshop.

"You sneaky son-of-a-bitch!" Johnny Framingham texted. "Polar bear, my ass!"

"Who the hell is Horatio King anyway ☺?" Billy Hansen texted. "Never heard of him."

Soon enough, Theatermania.com, Broadwaystars.com, and Broadway.com had all picked up the story, as had Variety and the Hollywood Reporter. A fast and furious half-hour after his mother had woken him, Ben got a phone call from a reporter from Playbill.com requesting an interview. Ben did his best to describe his book and how he had come to send it to King.

"What would you say Horatio King is like as a collaborator?" the woman asked.

Ben found he could answer truthfully. "Wonderful."

"Word has it that he's quite profane in private."

That one, Ben answered less truthfully.

"Not at all."

It wasn't until an hour and a half after the phone call from his mother that Ben finally got through to King himself.

"You changed your mind," Ben said.

King chuckled, clearly enjoying just how much he had caught Ben off-guard. "I'm a grumpy old man, but not a complete asshole."

"But why?"

"Come over and I'll explain. And after I do that, I want to play you the music to your *Caramel Apple* lyric. I think I found the right tune."

Ben arrived at King's apartment an hour later. Shuffling into the living room, the old man opened the conversation with the last thing Ben might have expected.

"Sorry about the other night. I'm afraid I cock-blocked you."

Ben blinked. Had he heard correctly?

"*Cock-blocked*?"

"My texts," King grunted. "Last Friday night."

"Oh, those," Ben laughed.

"Yes, *those*!" By then King was at the mantle. He fiddled with one of his Tony's as though it were a security blanket. "Kept me up all night. Depressing! The old codger getting in the way of the young man's fun. I felt the need to apologize."

Ben was shocked. Was this why King had changed his mind and announced their collaboration?

"Don't worry about that," Ben said. "It all worked out."

King put the Tony back on the shelf and then shot Ben a relieved glance. "It did? You're sure?"

In truth, Ben and Mo had texted just once over the weekend.

"We'll probably hang again."

King scowled. "Hang again? Is that what your generation calls intimate relations? Hanging?"

Ben shrugged. "I guess." Then he smiled.

"What?" King asked.

"If you want to know the truth, we were interrupted," Ben

76

said. "And not by you, either."

"Not by me?" King said. "By who then?"

"More like by what," Ben said.

"A what?"

"A raccoon."

King's eyes went wide, laced with horror. "My God, boy! Your generation is even kinkier than I thought. You have a pet raccoon?"

"Not a pet," Ben said with a laugh. "It lives under the kitchen sink. Down in the basement, I guess."

"Really now?" King said. "So this raccoon? It came to visit at an inopportune moment?"

"You might say that," Ben said. "My roommate had to chase it away with a broom."

"This is better than Amazon Prime," King said, shuffling toward Ben. "Where was your girl all this time?"

Ben grinned. What else could he do? "Under my blankets getting dressed."

King leaned on his cane and laughed out loud. "I like this girl. Sensible souls draw the line at live rodents."

"That's what she said," Ben said, laughing himself.

"So you're really going to see her again?" King asked.

"I hope," Ben said. "She leaves town in a month and I have to de-rodentize the apartment first."

"Good thought," King said, now moving toward the sofa and chair. "What's her name anyway? You didn't mention?"

"Mo."

"Mo, eh? As in *Maureen,* I imagine?"

"I think so," Ben said. "I honestly didn't ask."

"Must be," King said, plopping back into his customary chair. "Irish Catholic girl." He nodded to himself and chewed briefly on his beard. "You know, the Catholic girl, Jewish boy dichotomy often works well."

Ben didn't know whether to be offended or intrigued – maybe a little bit of both.

"Actually, I don't know what religion Mo is. And I'm only half Jewish and pretty lapsed."

"Half is close enough," King said. "It's the whole Bridget loves Bernie thing. Religions of outcasts – naturally, the Jewish boy is attracted to a shiksa. Unless he likes boys, of course."

Ben conceded the point. "Yes, if I was gay I wouldn't be trying to go to bed with a girl, that's for sure."

King waved a hand and then took a drink from a glass of water. "It's just as well."

"Just as well? What do you mean?"

"That you aren't gay, of course."

"Why?" Ben said. "My gay friends seem just as happy as my straight. Happier in some cases."

"Good to hear it," King said. Juniper took a chance and jumped into his lap. "Back in my day, being gay wasn't as easy."

As if to reassure him, Juniper licked the old man's beard, a gesture rewarded by King roughly patting his head.

"I wasn't even in love until I was forty," King went on, taking a quick sip of water, "though you probably know that."

Like all musical theater fans, Ben did know about King's love life. There was no use denying it.

"I got a lot of action, of course," King continued. "I didn't used to be so bad looking before I grew this atrocious beard. You've seen the pictures."

"Sure," Ben said. "You looked great."

It was true. Ben particularly remembered a handsome shot of a young King, no more than thirty, dressed in a coat and tie at the opening night party of *Madame Bovary*, one of his first hits. It now hung in Sardis.

King smiled. "I had some fun, that's for sure."

His voice trailed off, remembering. Then he took another drink of water – which is when Ben wondered if just maybe it wasn't entirely water at all, but laced with *something* – tequila? Vodka? Rum? Why else was he being so forthcoming? But whatever the reason, Ben's curiosity had gotten the better of him.

"So," he began. "Are you...?".

He paused. King laughed.

"Come on, boy. Out with it. What do you want to know?"

"Are you seeing anyone now? Sorry, none of my business."

"No, no, you're entitled to ask I suppose. Especially after I grilled you about Maureen. Especially after my royal cock-blocking."

Ben didn't quite see the logic but was glad to have permission to continue.

"There was a guy you were in love with fifteen or so years ago?" he asked. "Richard Sinclair, right?"

"Congratulations!" King roared. He stood up and took a little bow. "You've read my biography." He sighed, then muttered half to himself. "I knew I shouldn't have been so honest with that wench."

"Wench?"

It wasn't a word Ben heard bandied about.

"Yes, the writer," King said. He began to pace, planting his cane wildly before him. "She interviewed me for hours. Asked about my work, of course. My crazy father. But the sneaky thing would wait until the end of the session when I was tired then zero in on my love life. I was involved with Richard then."

"He's the actor, right?"

King nodded. "So I made the mistake of opening my big yap and saying I was in love." King shuddered. "Now it's all in disgusting print for everyone to see. Worse, I haven't seen Richard in years."

"What happened?" Ben asked. "You grew apart? That's what the book implied."

"Grew apart?" King growled. "I wish! No, the problem was me. I cheated!"

"Cheated?"

Ben was surprised. Even though King was the star, he had expected it to be the other way around – that Richard, a younger man, had found someone his own age.

"I told you I wasn't bad looking before my wrinkles went exponential," King said. "Even at seventy, I had a certain salt and pepper flair. Anyway, there was a fight. To be honest, Richard and I weren't really getting along. You try and act interested in the sides for someone's new sitcom for hours on end and see how long you last. He was getting dull and I had a fling. With who doesn't matter. Some punk. Given who I am, word spread. The price of fame, my boy. You can't get a decent fuck without everyone knowing. When Richard found out, the poor man was hurt, of course. Came to me crying. I cried, too, I'm not ashamed to admit. I did love him."

"Are you still in touch?" Ben asked.

King sighed. "I tried a year later right when his show *Love Me or Leave Me* blew up, but no reply. Can't say I blame him. He got famous and I'm a handful."

The two were quiet for a minute. A pigeon landed on the windowsill, pecked at something, then flew off. King took it as an excuse to wander to the window and look outside.

"That's all over," he said with a sigh then turned to Ben. "I mean, who would have this desiccated bag of skin and bones now?"

"Oh, I don't know," Ben began.

"Oh, sure, I can get it up," King went on, almost to himself. "But with more effort than I'd care to admit. Even assuming the sexual side of things worked out, you may have noticed that I'm a little bit too set in my ways and words to make for a good relationship. No," he said with finality. "My romantic days are done." He smiled. "Which means I'll have to live vicariously through yours. And once this show is a hit, you can move to a raccoon-free zone and invite over whatever Irish Catholic girl you'd like to bone – an entire army of them."

Ben let the last comment pass. But something else King said had caught his attention. And he had to ask. It was a stupid question, really, because Ben knew full well there was no possible answer.

"So…do you really think the show will be…a hit?"

King walked back to his chair and smiled with something actually approaching kindness.

"A hit?" The old man sighed. "I wish I knew, boy. A musical about a dessert contest? Sounds preposterous, right? Because it is! Oh, sure, the first articles have been nice enough, but trust me – everyone is secretly waiting for it to blow up in our faces. But fuck them, right? Family-themed shows have made millions. Most of them are bad. And ours? Well, I think it's going to be tremendous. That being said, I have no idea. Don't forget, I'm the guy who bet the bank on *Black Hawk Down*. In any case," he said, finally glancing at Ben's new lyric. "No other musical I can think of has a comic song about a man with an apple stuck to his face, am I right?"

Ben nodded. "That's true. We're certainly original."

"That we are," King said. "Which is what occurred to me last night. I got thinking: the kid is right. He deserves to tell everyone he knows what he's doing. Even everyone in that asinine songwriting class. And as for me? I have to get my head out of my ass and take ownership of this as my new project. Make sense?"

Ben nodded. "Yeah, sure. Thank you."

"Shut up," King said. "I should be thanking you. Don't forget, boy, this is my comeback, as it were. My last act. I might as well grab it by the balls."

Ben nodded. "I see."

But King wasn't through. "But when I grab something by the balls, I grab and hold on, son."

Ben swallowed. "Okay…"

"What I'm saying is I won't have it screwed up by a young guy who is more interested in tail than writing."

Ben blinked. "Wait. Is this about Mo, again?"

King nodded. "Yes, it's about *Maureen* and the raccoon and whatever other kinky stuff you're into. You see, now that I've announced our collaboration to the press my ass is truly on the line. Do you think we've been working hard before? Well, I've got news for you. We're about to work even harder. I have plans for this show. I'm already in touch with a few directors. I have my eye on Gwendolyn Bankhead. You've heard of her, of course?"

Of course. She was one of the hottest directors in the city, having won a Tony three years earlier for a daring staging of Arthur Miller's *The Crucible* using giant puppets.

"Wow," Ben said. "Would she be interested?"

"I'm still Horatio King, am I not?" the old man stated. "And if Gwendolyn is too busy, there are others. Mark D'Angelo.

Helen Wheeler. Fredericka Monclair. They'll fight for the chance to work with us."

Ben shuddered. Famous names all.

"Hell," King went on with a smile. "Everett Walker has been begging to direct me for years."

Ben blinked. Head of the National Theater in London, Walker was known for his unusual re-workings of Shakespeare. His most recent production of *Much Ado About Nothing* featured the cast costumed as animals.

"You think he's right for us?"

King shrugged. "Probably not. He's a weirdo. But my point is that we have a list. We'll get a first-rate director. And as for producers, well, they're mostly ineffectual pinheads who couldn't raise a lousy twenty K without crying to their daddies. But there are one or two I trust. And I can co-produce, too."

Ben blinked. "You will? Put in your own money?"

"What the fuck else am I going to do with it?" King said with a laugh. "Open a hot yoga spa? I'm damned rich with no immediate family. Why not spend a little of it on what I love?" Now King took a step toward Ben. "So you see, my young friend, your little letter to me a month ago has stirred up a giant hornet's nest. Are you up to the task?"

Ben swallowed hard.

"What are you saying? No girls?"

King laughed. "For a while anyway. Then you can fuck whoever you want. Writing first."

"Fine," Ben said. "Writing first. But does that go for you, too?"

"Writing before sex?" King said. "Didn't I just tell you I can barely get it up?"

"Not that," Ben said. He paused, then nodded at King's

water bottle. "Writing before drinking?"

King scowled then grinned. "Damnit, boy. You have read my biography."

Ben smiled sheepishly. "Only three or four times."

"It's published overseas, too," King said. "Read it a fifth in Sanskrit. All right, then. Yes, writing before drinking though my drinking problem isn't a problem anymore. After *Black Hawk* I was in rehab, though I assume you know that, too."

Ben nodded. He knew that, too.

"Isn't there alcohol in your water bottle?"

King held up the bottle. "This? Ha! Sip it yourself if you want. Pure, unadulterated H2O. My current garrulousness has to do with my natural disposition and the single adult beverage I had at lunch. Don't worry, kid. I'm not lacing my water bottle. You aren't going to weasel out of this collaboration by calling me an alcoholic. My mind is all there, and I promise to show up to work sober. Deal?"

He extended his hand. Ben took it. They shook.

"Deal."

"Writing before ass and alcohol."

Ben laughed. "Yep. Sounds fair."

"Good then," King said. "Now come. There's a song about a caramel apple crying out to be finished."

9

Horatio King had spoken too soon. Not about his drinking–that he was able to tamp down. It was his assertion that a stream of top-flight directors would fight for the chance to helm the now entitled, *Just Desserts* that turned out to be premature. That night, King sent the plot synopsis and two songs to Gwendolyn Bankhead. She was the first to decline.

"Dear Horatio," she emailed the next morning. "Your new show sounds *charmant*! But do you really think I'm the right lady to direct an ensemble of skating apple pies? Yes, my *Crucible* used occasional puppetry, but perhaps you need someone a bit zanier?"

"She might be right, actually," King muttered. "Our show needs a light touch." He stroked his beard. "*Hmmm*...how does Mark D'Angelo sound?"

Ben was awe-struck. Everyone knew about D'Angelo's staging of Rodgers and Hammerstein's *The Sound of Music*, updated to a modern-day dystopic America. Raves all around.

"Fine," Ben said. "But he's pretty dark. Will he be zany enough for us?"

King waved a hand. "Mark can do anything."

Including being the next to reject the show. It turned out that Ben's instinct was right.

"This material is too frivolous for me," D'Angelo informed the two collaborators over lunch later that week.

"Frivolous?" King said, doing his best to remain composed.

"You heard me," D'Angelo replied. "From what I've read your show is like a big apple pie. Sweet enough on the outside, but unadulterated goop beneath the crust."

"Fuck him," King told Ben after D'Angelo had abruptly marched out. "He's a pretentious shit anyway. And his dystopic *Sound of Music* was a mixed bag. Maria should've sung *My Favorite Things* with the children, not that gaggle of prostitutes."

When Fredericka Monclair said she was suddenly tied up in Berlin for the next year directing Shakespeare's history plays in German, an offer went to Helen Wheeler who was interested – very much so. Unfortunately, she was recovering from a rare health crisis brought on by too much drinking: a severe case of gout. Then the worst happened: Henry Twiddle, theater columnist for *The New York Post*, penned a Friday morning tidbit that speculated with some accuracy that "despite Horatio King's enormous talent, after the disaster that was *Black Hawk Down*, no right-minded director seems willing to take a chance on a musical that features a first-time book writer-lyricist and roller-blading apple pies."

"The bastard can't even get his facts right," King groused to Ben. It was over the weekend, Saturday evening. "The pies don't roller-blade. They roller-skate!"

Ben nodded. He had noticed the mistake, too, of course. But minor misinformation was the least of their problems.

"The right person will come along eventually, right?"

King pushed Juniper out of the way and collapsed on the sofa.

"Of course," King said. "But now that I think it over, maybe we've rushed it."

"Rushed it?"

"Yes. Perhaps we put our directorial search on hold for a

while, *hmmm*? Write more material so we have more to show. Sound like a plan?"

Ben nodded. As a novice, what other choice did he have but to trust the great King?

And so the hard work truly began. With a leave of absence from garbage photography (given the news of the new team *Willis and King*, Ben's mother agreed to fully subsidize him for a few months), the collaborators began at ten in the morning and went with only short breaks until ten at night, sometimes later. Ben's mind was soon a blur of caramel apples, flying pies, and rhyming citizens. He wrote lyric after lyric then crossed out word after word, his thumb soon moving instinctively to the rhyming app on his phone.

As the days stretched to weeks, both men learned to tolerate each other's quirks. A creature of habit, King paced when he worked, planting his cane heavily into the carpet. When an idea struck, he hustled to the piano, played and cursed, then cursed some more. Being elderly, he liked an afternoon nap, usually laid out in his chair in the living room, head back, mouth agape, Juniper, safe at last, on his lap. As for Ben, King soon learned that despite his new partner's youth, he liked to nap too, often at a moment's notice, usually on the floor. Like clockwork, Ben woke hungry. Within days, King was forced to give him free reign over his fridge. Ben also took free rein of the piano, an indulgence that drove King to the brink of insanity. Though Ben handled standards by Gershwin and Rodgers by ear with flair, he stumbled on newer music. One day, after enduring several egregious harmonic miscues on King's own *Lear*, the old man reached the end of his rope.

"Continue to massacre my music," he informed Ben. "And I shave your balls."

A month down the road the team put the finishing touches on Act One, a grand finale in which Applefeller and his assistant Samantha fly on an apple soufflé balloon to Iambia, the rhyming land in search of Captain B. Rollie Ragoon.

"Do you realize what this means?" King called from the piano. "Act One will end with a giant balloon coming down from the theater ceiling. The audience will have a collective orgasm."

"Every show these days needs big moments," Ben agreed. "Why not a flying soufflé?"

By early December, the writers were into Act Two, tackling a curtain opener showing Applefeller's arrival in Iambia. Then it was time for the biggest production number in the show. After Sylvester Sweet steals the Ragoon and Applefeller's roller-skating pies, he enters them as his own. The judges are ecstatic. The dessert grounds shake with excitement. After two days of work, Ben had a rough lyric. The first verse went like this:

Chorus: (singing joyously)
Rol-ler Skate! Rol-ler Skate!

Sweet:
Black tuxedos, red bowties.
Meet my roller-skating pies.
Everyone a taste delight resting in a tin.

Reporter:
Should we simple taste them cold?

Reporter Two:
Should we wait until they've rolled?

Sweet:
Wait until they've raced,
It enhances the taste.

For research has recently proved.
Those pastries on the go.
Have extra flavor.
And apple dessert that has moved.
Is thusly a dessert.
That one should savor!

Faster than a bat can blink.
Faster than a cat can slink,
Soon they'll be maneuvering the rink.
Oh, eyes'll open wide,
When they start to glide.
The kind of thrill one never could outgrow.
Captivating, figure-eighting, skating apple pies!
Ready or not – off they go!

Ben was proud of the lyric playfulness – so proud that, with King's grudging permission, he returned to the AMI workshop to share it with the class. This was just before Christmas. His first time back since his collaboration had been made public, Ben was greeted with equal doses of good cheer and barely veiled jealousy. After sharing the lyrics to a round of appreciative applause and comments, the class made a circle around him. The questions came fast and furious.

"What's he like?"

"Does he look as old as his pictures?"

"I hear his cane is made of a rare oak from Brazil."

"Can he still play piano?"

"Does he really beat his dog?"

"Is he an alcoholic or just a drunk?"

Then finally, the question that stopped everyone short. From Ethan Hancock.

"No offense, Ben. But how did you get him to work with you?"

Ben drew in a sharp breath. The class went silent. After all, it was a valid point. Why *had* the great King chosen Ben Willis to come out of retirement? That's when Jen Rosenthal came to Ben's rescue.

"Because his book is frigging great," she said. "If more people here had bothered to read it except me, you'd know."

Duly chastised, the class went silent. Ben stole a thankful glance at Jen. She smiled. Even so, Ben wasn't off the hook. Despite Jen's spirited defense, the class still wanted to know: how had it all happened? With requisite hemming and hawing, Ben finally explained.

"Late this August my roommate and I got really drunk. I found myself typing a late-night letter to Horatio King."

When the story was finished, Ethan Hancock said something surprising. "Well, now that you two are working together, why don't you invite him into class? I'm sure the students would love to meet him. You could share some of your work together."

Given King's reaction to the workshop in general and Ethan Hancock in particular, Ben seriously doubted that the great man would ever want to attend. He was right.

"Ethan invited me to the workshop?" King said the next

morning at his apartment. "Imagine that!"

"I assume you'd never go. From what you've said, I doubt you'd want to see Ethan anyway."

King waved a hand. "You're right. The little shit wanted to write with me once."

"Really?" Ben asked. This was news. "You never said."

"That's right," King said. "Came to me with an idea about a musical based on Proust. We even wrote half a dozen songs or so, but eventually, I told him to piss off. Because Ethan Hancock is nothing more than a hack. A talented hack to be sure – he's got skills – but a hack nonetheless."

"You really think?"

King grimaced. "Listen to his score from *Stepping Out* again. Porter mixed with a little Sondheim and a dash of King."

Ben smiled. In truth, he had admired *Stepping Out*.

"You saying he stole from you?"

"Let's just say heavily influenced. Whatever, that's all past."

"So you'd consider coming to class?"

King shrugged. "Me? At a songwriting workshop?" He laughed. "I think not. But I am interested. They wanted every detail, huh? I mean, about me?"

"Right."

"Bet they wanted to know how often I get up to piss."

"Well…almost."

"Probably wanted to know if I can still jerk off."

"No one asked."

King smiled. "It's just as well you went back to class, I guess. We all need a little ego boost now and then."

Ben shrugged, then smiled. "Yeah," he said. "I guess that part was nice."

"Good," King said. "Now listen. I need to tell you

something…there's been news."

"What?" Ben asked. "Something good, I hope?"

King patted him on the knee. "Possibly very good. Let me start at the beginning. You see, I was secretly hoping that Helen Wheeler might still direct for us."

"And…?" Ben asked.

King sighed. "I didn't want to get your hopes up, but last week I went over to see her."

"How's her big toe?" Ben asked.

King shook his head. "Her gout has taken a turn. The poor lady is in bed with both feet in a sling."

Ben grimaced.

"You know," he said. "Just to say it, I have a friend who I met at the Musical Theater Barn two summers ago. Natalie French. She's only in her early thirties but she's got lots of credits. Tons of musical theater. Assisting on Broadway, too."

"Assisting on Broadway, eh?" King said.

"Should we call her in for an interview?" Ben asked.

King shook his head. "Not yet."

"Why?"

"If you really like her, she could possibly assist whoever we hire, I suppose."

"She's out of the running? Just like that?"

Ben felt strangely disappointed. He didn't know Natalie well, that was true, but he liked the idea of giving her a chance.

"Sorry, son," King said, rising to his feet. "As talented as this Natalie may be, this is a new musical. There is more to manage than you can imagine: rewrites, sets, lights, the press, not to mention staging the damned thing. The whole ball of wax. We need someone who's been to the dance before, someone with experience."

Ben nodded. He had to admit it made sense.

"So who then? What? Did Everett Walker call?"

King nodded. "As a matter of fact, he emailed me two days ago."

"So?" Ben asked.

King frowned. "He's interested but let's not forget: his last production featured *Hamlet* on the International Space Station. Polonius was a Romulan."

"Oh, God," Ben said. "That sounds too weird, even for us."

"Agreed," King went on. "But wipe that pout off your face. This is what I've been trying to tell you. I have another lead. A good one this time."

"Someone who doesn't have gout, I hope."

"As far as I know."

"Who then?" Ben asked.

He couldn't think of a single new A-list candidate. Had Gwendolyn Bankhead decided she was zany enough after all? Had Mark D'Angelo reconsidered? But Ben would have to wait another minute. For just as King was about to utter the magical name, his cell phone rang. Instinctively, he glanced at the caller ID.

"Ah, ha," he said. "This might be who we've been waiting for."

King stood up. Leaning on his cane, he held his phone to his ear. Ben had no choice but to listen and wait.

"Yes, hello?" King said. "Hi there. No, no...thank you. The usual...hobbling around as best I can. So what say you?" King paused, then frowned. "Really now? You're sure? That bad, eh? Well, okay then. I guess we'll hope for next time. Yes, you, too."

With that, King clicked off with a muttered, "Fuck it."

"What?" Ben asked.

He didn't even know for absolutely sure if the phone call had to do with their directorial search – or with the show at all. Still, he had a sinking feeling. King plopped back on the couch.

"Oh, well," he sighed, giving Juniper a scratch. "Our search continues."

"What do you mean?" Ben said, sitting across from him. "Who was that?"

King forced a smile. "That? Not important now, I suppose."

"It seemed important," Ben insisted. "Come on. Who?"

"If you must know," King replied. "It was Cassandra Simpson."

Ben blinked. "Cassandra Simpson?"

Known for a string of hits as both director and choreographer, Simpson – or "Simps" to the theatrical community – hadn't had a show up for even longer than King.

"I thought she was retired," Ben went on. "Only doing big movies."

"She was. Apparently, she wants back on Broadway."

"And she's interested?" Ben said, leaning forward. "In our show?"

He couldn't believe it. They hadn't even considered her.

"Don't look so surprised, boy. Yes, she is. I mean, she was. That's what I was going to tell you a few moments ago. Her agent contacted me last night."

Ben still found it hard to comprehend. "Cassandra Simpson wants to make her comeback with our show?"

"As I said, she did."

"What happened?" Ben asked.

King gave Juniper another quick scratch and then pushed her to the carpet.

"Sorry to say it, my boy… but… well… apparently, she read

your book."

Ben blinked. "You mean *The Worldwide Dessert Contest*?"

"Of course, *The Worldwide Dessert Contest*," King exclaimed. "You've written others I don't know about?"

"Well, no." Ben's heart was racing. "What? She didn't like it?"

"That's one way of putting it."

"What then?"

"She found it abhorrent."

Ben was thunderstruck. Though naturally self-effacing, he had developed quite an ego about his baby. He wasn't used to people disliking it.

"That's what she said? Abhorrent?"

King shrugged. "Well, the actual word was preposterous."

"Really?"

"Ah, yes – also puerile!"

Ben couldn't comprehend it. "She didn't like the rhyming land? The roller-skating pies?" He slumped back on the couch and closed his eyes. "This is awful."

Then he got an idea – desperate, yes – but for a split second, the answer.

"You do it," he said.

King laughed. "Me?"

"Why not? You directed a revival of *Moses and Me*, right?"

"That was centuries ago."

"No one knows our show better."

"Perhaps," King replied. "But no one would fuck it up more. Besides, directing is hard. I'm a temper tantrum away from a coronary as it is."

"But…"

"Sorry, son. That's a non-starter."

Ben sighed heavily. Should he bring up Natalie French again? Not when he knew he'd be shot down. Unable to help himself, Ben circled back to Cassandra Simpson.

"I can't believe she hated my book."

Now King laughed.

"What? You think it's funny?"

"Sort of," the old man said. He patted Ben's knee. "There are lots of haters out there, son. The world is full of 'em. If you're going to stay in the arts, you'd better get used to it."

"Yeah, I guess," Ben said. Then he couldn't resist. "Just as long as you still like it."

He felt embarrassed the moment the words were out of his mouth. Then again, wasn't insecurity part and parcel of being an artist? Luckily, King took it in stride.

"Don't worry about me," he said. "I'm not sure why but I love this cockamamie show. I love it from Applefeller's opening song to his apple pancake until the moment in Act Two when the roller-skating pies tremble in their crusts and soar into the fucking sky. I can't wait to see it staged."

Ben was relieved. Still, King's encouraging words made Cassandra Simpkins' rejection sting more, especially when she might have been the perfect person to make those very pies get airborne.

"So what next?" Ben asked.

King smiled. "Don't you know?"

Suddenly, Ben did – there was only one way forward.

"Keep writing, right?"

King nodded. "Precisely. And hope for the best. Now come. The finale! It needs our attention, don't you think?"

10

Ben all but collapsed into King's elevator. Yes, he and the old man had had a good writing session. Still, it was all too stressful. Suddenly, the show that had seemed so promising had hit a massive roadblock. Was it wrong to have assumed that a major director would want to work with them? Apparently. And now, with the famous Simps out of the running, what other A-list directors were even available? Ben didn't know. At that point, he was too upset to even think through a list of names. Powerless, all he could do now was hold on tight and hope for the best.

Hitting the street in a daze, Ben knew he needed to focus – and quickly. For after a solid month with virtually no feminine contact – barely more than a weekly "catch-up" phone call to Gretchen—he had broken down and asked Mo to meet for coffee. Though they had exchanged occasional texts, Ben had kept true to his promise to Horatio King and politely avoided her hints of getting together. But on the eve of her trip to London, enough had been enough. He had wanted to see her again.

For lack of anywhere else to meet, the couple had picked a Starbucks on the Upper West Side. Moving quickly across the park, Ben did his best to keep his mind off of Simps' devastating reaction by reminding himself of his glowing reviews.

"A charming concoction of words and rhymes!"

Wasn't that what the *School Library Journal* had said?

"Call this delicious!" Booklist had raved.

Reciting his reviews again and again (yes, he had them

memorized), Ben all but speed-walked, arriving at Starbucks early. With nothing else to do, he killed time sipping a coffee, looking out the window at the first light snow of the season, reminding himself of other high praise his baby had received. The hell with Cassandra Simpson! What did a has-been Hollywood director know about children's books anyway? Obviously, very little.

"So? How's our raccoon?"

Ben looked up. Suddenly, Mo was standing before him, holding a latte. Ben's focus shifted, immediately regretting having let the fledgling relationship die off. Mo exuded a sweet swagger he found deeply appealing, that and the red lipstick and turquoise fingernails.

"Under control, actually," Ben managed. "I heard a squeak the other night, but it was just the fridge acting up."

In truth, Harrison had finally taken control of the situation, hiring someone to patch the holes behind the kitchen cupboard. He had also called an exterminator.

"Well, that's better," Mo said. "I prefer faulty electronics to live rodents."

There was a pause. Ben was suddenly nervous, unable to think of a single way forward out of the thousands of thoughts in his head. Luckily, Mo was more poised.

"And Horatio King?" she asked, taking a seat. "How's he doing?"

"Same as ever," Ben said quickly. Though dating protocol called for positivity, he found himself blurting out the primary thing on his mind. "We're looking for a director now."

"Ah, cool. Any leads?"

Ben shook his head. "Mostly a lot of people who've turned us down."

"Yeah," Mo said. "I read that."

Ben forced a grin. "One had gout."

"That hurts."

Ben looked out the window, then back at Mo. Why not admit it?

"Cassandra Simpkins hated the book."

Mo looked honestly surprised. "Really? Your book? Cassandra Simpkins?"

"Hated it," Ben repeated. "Called the story preposterous."

"God, sorry."

"Yeah, sucks."

Mo forced a smile. "Well, she's obviously insane. Who else would call herself *Simps*?"

Ben appreciated the sentiment. "Thanks."

"But, wait," Mo said. "Didn't I read that Everett Walker might be interested? The weird Shakespeare guy?"

"He is," Ben said. "But apparently he's *too* weird."

Mo shrugged. "You never know."

"What do you mean?"

"Your show is weird, too, isn't it? It might be a match."

Ben shrugged. With that, they hid behind sips of their drinks. Ben was about to fill the gap, saying something about the turning weather of all things when Mo reached into her bag and pulled out a manuscript.

"So anyway…I brought this for you to read."

"Hey, nice," Ben said, happy for a change of subject. "Your Botswana Dystopia?"

"Right," Mo said. "Though it's getting a little bit more upbeat as I go."

"Great," Ben said. "Do you want notes or just enthusiasm?"

Mo shrugged. "A little bit of both?"

Ben nodded. "Got it."

He tucked the fifty or so pages into his knapsack. After another short pause, Mo apparently decided it was time to take official control of the conversation.

"So what's been going on anyway, Ben?"

He blinked.

"Going on?"

"Yeah," Mo continued. "What's wrong?"

Ben smiled, his heart suddenly pounding. "With your book, you mean? I haven't read it yet. Probably nothing."

"Not my book," Mo said. "You know I don't mean my book. Or your search for the right director. You're acting sort of guilt-ridden."

"Guilt-ridden?" Ben asked. "Really?"

"About our date, maybe?" she mused. "I had a good time that night." She added pointedly. "A month ago now."

Ben hadn't known what to expect from this meeting. Good conversation? Light banter? Maybe another shot at sex? Instead, Mo – to her credit – was zeroing directly in on what was really going on.

"We did." Ben met her eyes. "I did."

"So did I."

"I'm glad."

"Then why haven't we gotten together?" Mo asked, leaning forward. "You've avoided me, right?"

Ben sighed. He suddenly felt like a fool. Was the customary excuse "I've been caught up with work" sufficient? Probably not. But it was true. He had been caught up in work.

"Sorry to be so blunt," Mo went on, "but I'm a little bit sick of guys who jerk me around."

"Jerk you around?" Ben said. "That's the last thing I wanted to do."

Mo's eyes went wide. "Oh, really? Last week I recall sending you a text asking you for dinner at my place."

Ben nodded. Indeed, she had.

"Your answer was the vaguest thing I've ever read," Mo went on. "And I know it was intentional. I read your book. You can write." She paused. "I know it was only one date. But it was a good one."

"It was," Ben said. "I'm sorry about the weird response. I apologize for that, seriously. I'd love to go on another date with you."

"But what?" Mo asked. Her eyes went wide. "Ah, I know! Gretchen?"

"No," Ben said. He smiled. "That only kicks in when I'm forty-three and a half."

"But you are half in love with her."

Ben felt the blood rushing to his face. Was it really that transparent?

"Not really," he said. "Not anymore."

"Then what?" Mo asked. "Is there someone else?"

Ben found himself squirming. "Well, sort of. Actually…"

"Actually…who?"

Ben shifted uneasily in his seat, embarrassed. Then he spat it out: "Horatio King."

Mo blinked. "What?"

"You heard me."

Mo laughed. "You're gay?"

"No, no," Ben said. "Not gay. I'm a rare subset of males who write kids' books and musicals and are straight."

"So what does Horatio King have to do with it? What's the problem?"

"The problem," Ben said. He paused, feeling irredeemably stupid. "The problem," he began again. "Is that he made me take a blood oath not to date while we're writing the show. He's putting himself on the line, investing his own money, and he even vowed not to drink…"

Ben heard his voice trail off, realizing how profoundly stupid he must sound.

Mo laughed. "You're kidding!"

Ben shrugged.

"You avoided my invitation because you promised a grumpy old man?"

"Because I promised a genius," Ben found himself saying.

Why was he defending it? Then he remembered the other reason.

"Also, you're off to London," he said.

He was flailing, he knew. But it was true, wasn't it? What kind of future could they have?

Mo sighed. "I am going to London. But…"

"But what…?"

"I don't know, Ben. I don't meet many decent guys who I like even a little. So yeah, I'm going to London for six months or so and yeah, I left your apartment because I was spooked by a raccoon…but still, I thought maybe we could get to know each other before I go. But Horatio King! I mean, I've been dumped for all sorts of reasons but the bizarre demands of a crazy eighty-something is something new."

Ben paused. Suddenly, the truth of what he had done that month came crashing down on him. Why should he put his entire love life on hold just to write a musical? Even one for Broadway?

"Oh, God," Ben said. "I'm a moron."

Mo laughed. "You are."

Ben reached for her hand. She let him take it – for a brief second, then let it go.

"I do like you, Mo."

"I like you…I think."

Ben took her hand again. This time she let him hold it.

"Is it too late now?"

Mo grinned. "To what? See what you can get before I leave for Europe?"

Ben couldn't win. Then again, he knew he was playing the game poorly.

"Tell you what." Mo collected herself and smiled. "You read my book and work on your show. I'll go to London. We'll text and follow each other on Instagram. Then when I come back and Horatio King has made you a big star we can see where we stand. Deal?"

Ben paused. What choice did he have but to forget the whole thing or agree to terms?

"Deal," he said – but with a heavy sigh.

Anyway, it appeared to be the correct response. Mo gave Ben a kiss on the cheek, a gentle one. But then she stood up to go. She always seemed to be doing that. Maybe that's why Ben liked her so much.

"I'll be back before you know it and…we'll see what happens."

For a moment, Ben almost thought he was in love. He certainly considered running after her. But then he paused. Mo was right. The situation was unwinnable. No fool, Mo wasn't going to throw herself at him after he had admitted that he had struck a "no sex" deal with Horatio King. She had too much class. Their only hope was to wait and see.

"Hey, Mo," he heard himself calling.

At the doorway, she turned. "Yeah?"

"Have a good trip, okay?"

Mo smiled, maybe a bit sadly. "Good luck with the musical. I hope you find your director."

With that, she was out the door. With a heavy sigh, Ben drained his latte and walked into the falling snow.

The next day, Ben arrived at King's apartment promptly at ten, after a fretful night worrying that the old man had reconsidered their collaboration.

"You know what, son," Ben imagined King saying. "Maybe Simps has it right. Maybe the whole thing is just, well, a little bit too idiotic." Then King would chase him out the door, hurling another Tony at his head.

Instead, Ben found the door ajar. Letting himself into the foyer, he heard a voice echoing from the living room.

"It was absolutely astonishing."

"What was astonishing?" King replied.

"Just how bloody little was happening on that stage."

Ben drew in a sharp breath. A British accent? A rumbling bass? Who was it?

"It was dull beyond belief," the voice was saying now. "Whatever happened to pacing? Whatever happened to taste? To scenic integrity? There were so many things wrong, my head nearly fell off, just plop – right into my shirt. It was that bad."

"Well," King said. "The very idea of performing *Streetcar* in a spa seems like a damned bore anyway."

Ben took a step further down the hall and waited by the entrance to the living room. King was in his usual chair, Juniper lying on the armrest. A middle-aged man with a slight belly was leaning against the mantle. Ben had seen pictures from years earlier when the man was younger. Despite compensating for age with a streak of dyed black hair amidst a sea of gray, he was still handsome, if a bit rounder around the middle. His jowly face had a welcoming brightness. His green eyes went wide with childlike enthusiasm when he brought up a point.

"Everett Walker?" he whispered to himself. "What...?"

"It was a bore," the man went on. "Stanley gave his famous "Stella, Stella" speech covered in a beach towel, wearing light blue flip-flops. It was distracting. And they led Blanche off to the asylum at the end dressed in a pink bikini. Poor actress. Then again, maybe it helped. That outfit would drive anyone insane."

"But wait," King said. "You're the man famous for his *Much Ado About Nothing* in a barnyard with the cast costumed as animals."

Ben blinked. A barnyard? Yes, it had to be Everett Walker!

"That was different," he said.

"Why's that?"

Walker flashed a brilliant smile that left none of his teeth to the imagination. "Because it worked, that's why," he said. "Benedict was a natural rooster. Brilliant stuff, if I do say so myself."

King nodded. "That it was. But did you have to make Beatrice a pig? That was cruel. Not to mention sexist."

Walker waved a hand. "Pigs are the smartest animal at the farm. Second, this particular pig was gorgeous, the prize of all hogs. It was an intentional comment on the battle between the sexes, a role reversal, if you will."

King smiled. "Whatever you say."

"Critics are idiots," Walker sighed. "They missed the entire point."

King smiled. "A story for another day. But I believe we have company. Don't just stand there, boy," he called to Ben. "Come in. Meet Everett Walker."

Ben took a shy step into the room. Even though he had been working with King for a few months now, he was still prone to be star-struck. Despite being known for theater of the indisputably strange, Everett Walker was a genuine theatrical luminary. The sight of two giants together in the same room took Ben's breath away. Walker lurched toward him, hand outstretched.

"Excited to meet the brilliant author," he said, taking his hand. "Very excited, indeed."

Ben gasped. Brilliant? Is that what Everett Walker had just called him?

King nodded from the couch. "I took the liberty of describing some of the songs before you arrived."

"Okay…," Ben said.

"You see," King went on. "Everett took the liberty of flying himself into the city to meet us."

"You did?" Ben asked. "From England?"

"Of course!" Walker said. "I read your book on the trip across the pond."

Ben was shocked. "Really?"

He hoped he liked it more than Cassandra Simpkins.

Walker wagged his big head. "I always read the source material. Flying apple pies. Love it. The basis for a big, dark musical."

"Dark musical?" Ben asked.

"Not dark like *Lear*, of course," Walker said with a glance to King. "Not dark like Ibsen or O'Neill. But your piece does make a trenchant comment on the degradation of western society, does it not?"

"I suppose," Ben stammered. Was this guy for real? Was King really considering letting him direct? "Mostly, it's meant to be a story about one man's ability to persevere against all odds."

"Of course, it is," Walker said, wagging his head. "That's all there. I love your characters. John Applefeller is an everyman, is he not? A Forest Gump for the 21st Century, I should think – the simpleton, an innocent who somehow shows the others what's important about life. And his ten-year-old assistant, Samantha! We see the whole story through her innocent eyes. Ingenious!"

Actually, Ben could buy all that. "I suppose."

"Onto Judge Barkle!" Walker all but shouted it, pacing now, rubbing his hands together like a mad scientist. "I worship him in all his pompous glory. Pity about his caramel apple. But it's a metaphor and a brilliant one at that. Don't we all have our own respective caramel apples attached to our respective faces? Aren't we all struggling with some sort of manifest pain?"

"Of course we are," King shouted.

"Yes," Walker said wheeling around to briefly face King, then pivoting back to Ben. "And Sylvester Sweet," he went on, brushing a finger through his dyed hair. "What a fantastically, mischievous villain. He's utterly delicious! That scoundrel! Winning each year with his double-chocolate-fudge-raspberry-coconut-lime swirl! What's so wonderful is how you make the reader believe that it's really good. I mean, raspberries and limes? In a dessert? Sounds disgusting. Revolting! But you do it. You pull it off, my boy!"

"That he does," King shouted again, suddenly becoming Walker's cheering section. "Oh, how he does!"

By this point, Ben had let himself be flattered into submission. Praise this enthusiastic was hard to resist. And who would've guessed a short month ago that one of the world's most unusual directors would sing his praises? True, he was odd – very odd – but Walker seemed to get his work at the molecular level. And he wasn't done either, not by a longshot.

"Sweet is really a true egoist, is he not?" he said. "All that bluster? All those lies? Doesn't do anything on his own. A bona fide American villain. The self-made man. But he isn't self-made at all, is he? No! He's stolen everything from the Ragoon! Won every year with the Ragoon's dessert. Which brings me to the man himself. The Ragoon. Ah, but he's a delight. So spindly! A fucking rhyming gumby. I would die to choreograph his movement. I want to give him a big soul hug. Ah, those rhymes you've concocted. Brilliant!"

Then to Ben's absolute surprise, Walker looked dreamily across the room.

"Ah, here it comes," King said. "Have a seat, boy."

"What?" Ben asked.

"Have a seat!"

Ben did as he was told. Then to his utter shock, Walker began to speak. But not just any words. His words. The words of the Ragoon, one of his rhymed speeches, a response to a nosy reporter about what made him such a great dessert chef. Walker rolled his Rs and popped his Ts, enunciating as though he was reciting a Shakespearean monologue.

"How good am I?
Well, let me see.
Just as good as good can be.
Years ago, I thought I could
Never, ever be as good
As I am now but then again,

108

Maybe I was better then?
But if that's true, I've been a dunce.
To get less good than I was once.
So you see I'm in a jam.
It's hard to tell how good I am.
Then or now, now or then?
Repeat the question once again?"

When he was done, he took a moment to let the final words dissipate into the air, then shook himself and looked shyly around the room as though the effort had made him slightly woozy.

"Very nice," King said. "Remind me to set that speech to music."

Ben was still stunned.

"You memorized it?" he stammered.

It was as though he half expected that Walker would reveal that he had secretly written the text on his hand.

"Indeed," Walker said. "I try to memorize a new speech every day."

"Don't ask him to do *Hamlet*," King said. "We'll be here all night."

Walker laughed. "What's all night when devoted to Shakespeare?"

"Oh, do shut up," King said, playfully. "Shakespeare had his moments but is hardly worth all the fuss."

Walker's eyes went wide.

"That's the most preposterous thing I've ever heard. Shakespeare...?" Then he stopped, realizing that King was chuckling.

"For Christsake, Everett," King said. "You are so gullible. Of course, Shakespeare is great. None better." He winked at Ben.

"Except me. Now? Tell me, Ben? What do you think? Mr. Walker has flown himself all the way in from England to hear our show. Shall we to the study? Shall we play him Act One?"

Walker looked expectantly at Ben. Ben looked at King, trying to read his mind. What was he saying? That Walker should get the job?

"Well…," Ben began.

"Good! King said. "Let's play it."

Walker wagged his head. "Yes, yes," he cried, marching toward the study. "Act One. And whatever you have of Act Two, as well. I want to hear every word, every precious note!"

"I told you he was desperate to work with me," King whispered to Ben as Walker disappeared into the other room. "What do you think?"

"What do you think?" Ben replied.

King smiled. "He's an oddball, all right, but maybe I misjudged him. Damned impressive how he read the book, *hmmm*?"

Ben nodded. "It is – and that he liked it."

"He loved it," King exclaimed. "And there's another bonus. Everett will be very helpful in getting English producers."

Ben knew how important it was to raise money. But was this the right move? This was the man, after all, who had staged *Hamlet* in space.

"Just tell me that he's not going to set the thing on Venus," Ben asked. "That's all I ask."

King laughed. "Don't worry. I'll see that he doesn't." He yelled into the other room. "Everett! If we sign you on you must promise to set our show in the Appleton Dessert Grounds where it belongs. On the planet Earth, deal?"

A voice echoed back form the study. "I wouldn't think of

doing it anywhere else."

"No strange costuming, either!"

"Of course not!"

King looked to Ben. "So, my boy," he said. "What do you think? Do we take the risk?"

Ben nodded, slowly. "If you're in...then I guess we do."

"Good!" The old man draped an arm over Ben's shoulder. "Come, my boy. Smile! *Just Desserts* is on its way!" With that, he extended his cane and ambled quickly toward the study. "All right then, Everett," he cried. "We start with the overture!"

11

Two weeks later found Ben sitting in the backseat of a cab on his way to Kennedy Airport. It had been a heady time. Not only had he and King finished a rough draft of *Just Desserts* over the holidays, but Everett Walker had officially signed on to direct a workshop at the Public Theater in London.

"We'll fiddle with it across the pond this January in my neck of the woods," Walker had said. "That way we steer clear of the dear shits."

"Dear shits?" Ben had asked.

Walker and King smiled.

"You innocent," King said. "It's what we sometimes call the people who come to a new show hoping it'll be terrible so they can run home and tell their friends."

"And believe me," Walker said. "Word on the street is that we're already in trouble."

"Based on what?" Ben asked.

"My general strangeness," Walker said.

"Not to mention my recent past," King said. "Then there's your youth, our off-beat subject matter as well as the human proclivity, especially prevalent in the world of theater, for taking pleasure in seeing others crash and burn."

"Indeed," Everett Walker said. "Best to workshop our little baby out of town."

So it had been decided. *Just Desserts* would have its first hearing in London, an ocean away from the "dear shits."

Moving onto the Robert Kennedy Bridge, Ben allowed his mind to roam. The unexpected trip across the pond had another benefit, of course: Mo. True, they had left it that they would pick things up when she was back in New York. But didn't this sudden change of plans allow for an addendum to their agreement? Ben hoped so. He had tried to be a better friend, at least, taking time to read her manuscript and then writing an email of sincere praise. Mo replied with thanks. But aside from one more quick exchange, Ben had been focused on *Just Desserts*. In fact, he had been so busy – so consumed with the show – that he had only spoken to Gretchen twice, both times about an invite she had arranged for him to come to Vermont that spring as a visiting author at the officially designated Middlebury Chamber of Commerce and Agrarian Society Bookfair.

Now Ben looked out the cab window onto the busy Long Island Expressway and imagined the inevitable day – he couldn't resist – when the London workshop, a sterling success, led to Broadway; then his Tony nomination and winning speech in which he would thank everyone from his parents and Horatio King to Ruff-Ruff his childhood dog. Best of all, Ben envisioned the next day: how he would saunter into the AMI workshop like a Roman conqueror, toting his Tony for all to see. What a scene it would be! Johnny Framingham, Tiffany Holt, Steve Andrews – all of them – would salivate with envy, possibly even prostrate themselves on the floor. With admirable magnanimity, Ben would pass the prized award around the room, allowing his classmates to pretend, however briefly, that it was theirs. Some classmates would feign indifference but others – most of them – would shake with envy, shedding tears of genuine awe. Even Ethan Hancock would have no choice but to nod and say, "Nicely done, Willis. Nicely done."

It was a satisfying fantasy. But even while lost in thoughts so gratifying, Ben was smart enough to be aware of how fast life could turn. In truth, there was no guarantee that *Just Desserts* would get to Broadway, let alone win him a Tony. First, they had to circumvent the "dear shits" and get through the workshop. Who knew what could happen? Everett Walker might shroud the piece in a morass of pretension. Keeping with his barnyard theme, he might break his promise and costume John Applefeller as a giant fetal pig. And then there was King himself. He might return to drink or even drop dead.

Ben shuddered. It would be tragic to come so close only to have everything fall to pieces. And it *could* happen. Hadn't *Black Hawk Down* been a spectacular failure? Then again, *Black Hawk Down* was a musical about the Battle of Mogadishu with an Act Two opener called "The Somalia Night Boogie." *Just Desserts* was better than that! King and Walker had both said it: *The Worldwide Dessert Contest* was unusually fertile source material, a novel that had given birth to a show that could be experienced both as a brilliantly conceived light entertainment as well as a darker social commentary on modern-day America.

Just Desserts would be a hit. It had to be!

The traffic thickened. By the time Ben made it to the airport, he was running late. Hurrying into the terminal, he swiped his passport at a kiosk then looked around frantically.

"Flight 201 to Heathrow," he called to an agent, a young man in a British Airways uniform.

"Ticket, please."

Ben fumbled through his coat pocket and retrieved the severely crumpled boarding pass he had printed at home that morning. While the agent smoothed it out, Ben glanced to the security line – it was long, spilling out of the guardrails into the terminal.

"Really sorry," Ben said. "But I'm in a bit of a rush."

"No worries," the agent said. "This way, please."

He pointed up a stairway.

Ben blinked. "What's up there?"

"Business class lounge. Enjoy your flight."

Ben glanced again at his boarding pass and saw the giant "B." Of course – how could it be otherwise?

"Thank you," he said. He didn't know if he had ever felt so grateful about anything. "Thank you kindly."

"Cheerio."

Ben ran up the stairs. Moments later he cleared security. Then he flashed his boarding pass once again and was admitted to an elegant lounge, a seemingly haphazard arrangement of sofas, easy chairs, and coffee tables all in strategic proximity to the requisite bar. King was seated by the window, cradling a drink and speaking on a cell phone.

"Nice," he was saying as he waved Ben over. "So let me see if I've got this straight. We've got Jim Bunsen, the lazy fuck, as Sylvester Sweet, Danielle Fleming as Dentina, and Brian Schiflin as Applefeller. His high range is a bit of an adventure but he'll do."

King took a healthy swig from his drink, then covered the mouthpiece with his palm.

"Talking casting with Everett," he whispered. "Won't be a minute."

Ben didn't especially like being left out of the process but saw the logic. After all, with the workshop in England didn't it make sense for Walker to cast the show with local talent?

"Don't worry," King had promised. "No one will be

promised anything permanent. When we come to New York, we'll have a full slate of auditions, as usual."

Now King pulled lightly on his beard and barked into the receiver. "Just make sure you get someone who can rhyme like hell for the Ragoon. Someone who doesn't spit when they patter. Very good, Everett. Ben just arrived. Almost time to hop on the plane. See you tomorrow."

King clicked off.

"We're in good shape, I think."

"Oh?"

King nodded then took a healthy sip of his drink. "We've got a girl who can sing higher than the third moon of Jupiter to play Irma Frostina. And our Josiah Benson can practically belch a low C."

Ben smiled. The parts were written for a dramatic soprano and bass. "That works."

"Damn right, it does. Now come." King nodded to the bar. "What are you drinking?"

"Nothing yet."

King laughed. "Novice! Do you mean to tell me that you've been in a Business Class lounge for a full minute and aren't soused? And don't look at me that way. We're off working hours now so our little agreement is moot. Besides, I'm a nervous flier. It's either this…" He raised his glass. "Or a fistful of valium."

King drained his drink and handed it to Ben.

"Scotch on the rocks, please."

Ben smiled. What else was there to do? And why not celebrate? When was the last time he went on a European boondoggle? When would he ever go on a European boondoggle again? Probably never.

"Got it," Ben said and walked to the bar, returning moments

later with another scotch for King and a beer for himself.

"Life is strange, isn't it?" the old man said as Ben sank into an adjacent easy chair and took a swallow of beer.

"How so?"

"How so?" King replied. "Think of it, boy! A short time ago, I was trying to figure out whether or not I should bother finishing my memoirs or take Juniper out for his morning piss when you showed up, a callow youth with an absolutely absurd idea for a musical. A musical with skating apple pies, for fuck's sake. Who would have thought it?"

Ben smiled.

Yep. Life was strange.

King leaned forward and grinned. "Tell me. What did you really think when you came to visit me that day?"

"Honestly?" Ben asked. "Mostly I was worried you'd throw me out."

"Which I did, as I recall."

"*Lear*, right? I still have the scar."

"It's a badge of honor," King said. "Like a bad *Times* review."

Ben shuddered. A badge of honor he hoped never to earn. Just then, a voice crackled over the loudspeaker.

"Passengers on Flight 201, please proceed to Gate D 12 for boarding."

"That's us," King said. "Shall we?"

Ben helped the old man with his bag down the terminal to their assigned gate. They made an odd couple. With Ben toting two bags and King with his cane, a passerby would have been excused for mistaking them for a patient and his nurse. Slowly they navigated their way to Gate D 12.

"Fancy that," King said when they arrived. He gestured to

the Departure Board. "The goddamn thing is on time."

Before he could reply, Ben sensed a glimmer in his peripheral vision. Of course, King had hundreds of fans, one more ardent than the next – he knew that. But never before having been out with the great man in public, he hadn't experienced a so-called *Kingista* firsthand. Now one was lurching toward them.

"Mr. King?" she called. "Horatio King?"

Ben looked just in time to see a young woman, maybe a few years younger than him, approaching like a freight train.

"I saw you there and I thought, my God! It's Horatio King!"

If Ben was worried that the old man would show no more patience for a fan than his beleaguered dog – he half expected King to hit the young woman in the solar plexus with his cane and cry, "Piss off" – he was wrong. Used to the attention, and maybe even a little bit more pleased than he might be willing to admit, King nodded, kindly enough.

"Yes, it's me. The man himself."

An admission that set off a torrent.

"I thought it was you. I saw you there and I thought, 'Who is that?' and then I thought 'That's Horatio King!' and then I thought 'I have to speak to him.' I know you're about to get on a plane and everything but your music means everything to me. *Evergreen* is my favorite. After I saw it – this was in college – my roommate Bessie and I went back to our dorm, lay on the floor, and wept."

"Thank you, kindly. Now…"

"I was in *Twice Upon a Time* in high school," the woman went on, moving even closer. "I played Felicia. With a limp."

"Oh, really?" King said, glancing ever so quickly to Ben. "A limp?"

"To highlight her emotional pain. Oh, God. So, I have a

question, if that's okay. A friend of mine – Bessie, actually – has a bootleg from your musical of *In Dubious Battle.* 'Steinbeck, right?"

Now it was Ben's turn to be surprised.

"You wrote a musical based on *In Dubious Battle?*"

"Nothing you would have heard of," King said. "It died in workshop."

Ben shuddered. The idea of something "dying in workshop" was the last thing he wanted to hear.

"It did?"

"I loved the songs I heard," the young woman went on.

King waved a hand. "Sorry, my dear. That was pure shit."

The girl looked stricken. "No."

King nodded. "Afraid so. That was me trying to write a country score – disastrous." He turned to Ben. "It was so bad it didn't even make more than a single sentence in that rancid biography you read." Then back to the girl. "If your Bessie still has a bootleg, kindly ask her to burn it."

Unsure how to respond, the woman brought out a piece of paper and pen.

King scrawled his signature. Then, to Ben's surprise, the old man handed the paper to him.

"If you're smart, you'll get this young man's, too. My new book writer, Ben Willis."

The woman met Ben's eyes. "I read about it in *Broadwaystars.* Are you working on the show in London?"

"If we survive the flight. Sign, Ben. We have a plane."

Ben had signed copies of his book at schools, but this was the first time he had ever given an actual autograph. Not knowing precisely what to write, he penned his name then added a scrawled, "Thank You."

"No, thank you," the woman said. She snapped a picture of the two collaborators on her cell phone. "Thank you so much."

Holding the paper like a sacred artifact, she disappeared into the terminal rush.

Ben shuddered.

"What's wrong, boy?" King asked. "She's just a fan. A relatively charming one at that."

Ben swallowed hard. "What you said about *In Dubious Battle* dying in workshop." He paused, unable to resist asking the unanswerable question. "That's not going to happen to us, right?"

"Ah, is that what's bothering you?" To Ben's surprise, King threw him a look that almost approached affection. Then he put an arm around his shoulder. "Remember what the wise man said, son. We're like barnacles in the sea. All we can do is float with the tide and hope for a good ride."

Ben had wanted solid reassurance, not philosophy. "Damn straight our show is coming to New York," he wanted King to exclaim. "I guarantee it!" But Ben knew not to push the matter. King wasn't going to throw him a more optimistic crumb, not now anyway.

"Ah, look," the old man said. "A miracle."

"What?" Ben said, hoping for another encouraging word about the show's future.

"We're boarding. Come."

Ben had only flown Business Class once before, a domestic flight to Florida. Though it had been nice – a little more leg room and a drink or two – it had been nothing special. But British Airways overseas was a different story. There were six large seats per row, each one with a screen and a console that promised an unlimited horizon of movies and TV shows.

"Whoa," Ben said as the collaborators took the left turn from the plane's door.

"Wait," King replied. "There's more."

"Ah, Mr. King," the flight attendant said. "Right this way, please."

King winked at Ben. "Watch this."

"Watch what?"

"As per your request," the attendant said. "You've been upgraded."

"Upgraded?" Ben said.

"Yes, please follow me."

Astonished, Ben followed King down the aisle. Then the attendant swept away another curtain. First class! Four seats across, each one its own little pod, complete with videos, music, comfort, and around-the-clock wait service.

"Good enough?" King asked.

"You sure this is, okay?" Ben stammered.

King laughed. "Sit!"

A moment later the collaborators were seated side by side, King with another scotch while Ben sipped a coke with lime, overlooking the entertainment options. One pre-takeoff drink turned into another, and then just like that they were airborne. After a perfectly acceptable meal with champagne, Ben reclined in his seat and began to watch a movie while King slurped yet another drink, wobbled to the bathroom, then settled into a video as well. As the sky outside turned dark, the stewards dimmed the lights. Ben dozed off and then fell into a surprisingly deep sleep. Little did he know that the trip was about to become more dramatic. An hour later, Ben woke abruptly. Someone was shaking his arm – and shaking it hard. That someone was King.

"Damnit to hell. Look at it!"

"Huh?" Ben said.

King's eyes were wide with horror.

"It's a disgrace, I tell you."

Ben looked groggily to his right.

"A disgrace? Hey, are you okay?"

"Okay?" King slurred the word. The few drinks had clearly multiplied. "How can I be okay when faced with this mon…this mon…this monstrosity?"

Ben finally realized that King was gesturing to the video screen. Was it an old movie? TV show? An elegant elderly man was on screen, addressing a middle-aged woman – his daughter perhaps.

Then it clicked.

"Oh, God," Ben said. "You didn't."

"I most certainly did!"

It was an early episode of *Love Me or Leave Me*. The actor was Richard Sinclair.

King's Richard!

"Why are you watching that?"

"Couldn't sleep," King exclaimed, too loudly. "I was scrolling through channels and there it was."

"Is it that bad?" Ben asked.

"That bad?" King exclaimed. "Wasting one's life on the idiot box? On a *Situation Comedy*? Christ Almighty! The man should be doing Shakespeare!" To Ben's horror, the old man suddenly lurched to his feet and faced the rest of first class. "Shakespeare, damn it!"

Ben quickly guided King back to his seat. This was more serious than he had thought.

"Shhhh! People are trying to sleep."

"Well, I'm trying to talk," King said. "Richard Sinclair had talent. The kind of talent that comes around once in a generation."

"If it's bugging you, just turn it off."

Ben reached for King's video controls. King grabbed his arm in an iron grip.

"I never told you who I left Richard for, did I? Why I cheated?"

That prized information hadn't even made it into King's biography.

"No."

"Don't you want to know, boy?"

"Well…"

Ben wasn't sure that he did. King leaned even closer. Ben nearly gagged on his breath: pure scotch.

"*Ethan Hancock.*"

Ben blinked.

"What?"

"You heard me!" Just like that, King was back on his feet, facing the other passengers. "Ethan Fucking Hancock!"

"Please, Mr. King," the Steward called.

Again, Ben guided King back to his seat.

"Shhh, it's all right."

"It most certainly is not!" King whispered sharply. "It is not all right at all. I messed things up with Richard for a quick roll in the hay with a piece of musical comedy mediocrity."

"I thought you said Richard was boring."

"That's what a relationship is sometimes, right? Oh, you're too young to know. You're just a boy who can't say no, a serial monogamist!"

"Hey," Ben began.

"You've never been in love," King interrupted, again slurring his words. "Maybe you think you have but not really.

No, it's okay, boy, you just aren't ready. What I had with Richard was deep. Deep, man! We'd spend nights talking about Copland! Pinter! Liza Fucking Minnelli! And I blew it. The question is 'why?' The old man drained his drink. How many had he had? Four? Five? *Six*? "Why?"

Ben knew that he was out of his league. King was right: What did he know about love? Still, he had to try.

"Relationships end, right?" Ben said, lamely.

King scowled. "That's all you have for me? Relationships end? I knew you were young, but what is this? Sesame Street? I didn't want to leave him, don't you see? That was never my goddamned intent. I only wanted to cheat. Have a little fun."

"How did you even meet Ethan?" Ben asked. "You never said."

"Like I meet everyone," King stuttered. He shook his head and blew his nose, loudly. "The fucker wrote me a letter. Said he was a fan. Said he wanted to meet me."

Suddenly, the old man was again on his feet.

"Wanted to meet the great King! Wanted to write a show about Proust!"

"Shhh!" Ben said, pulling him back down to the seat. Several passengers stirred in their sleep, and one, a middle-aged man with an ample belly, smiled broadly, clearly enjoying the show.

"What?" King barked.

"Quiet. Inside voice."

"Wanted to meet me," King whispered sharply, leaning heavily toward Ben. "I said yes. I'm good that way sometimes. Wanting to help the younger generation. So Ethan came over. He's a fake but he has a certain charm. Lean and nice-looking – and he flattered me, of course. They all do. We hit it off. Talked about fly fishing for fuck's sake."

"Fly fishing?"

"I grew up going to the Berkshires in the summer, fishing in ponds and creeks. What? You're surprised?"

"A little."

"There's lots of shit I've done in my life you don't know about."

"Okay, okay," Ben said. "So you hit it off."

"We did. I invited him to my cabin upstate. He said yes. They all did. I told you I was a bit of a looker back then. Even at age seventy. Christ, boy, I'm Horatio King. They all wanted me."

"Where was Richard during all of this?" Ben asked.

"Out west, pilot season, auditioning for a precursor to this dreadful show."

"Father and Sunshine?" Ben asked.

King shuddered. "Yes, another *Situation Comedy*, that one about a man and his pet animatronic ape." King shook himself. "Richard had the goods! His Hamlet could make a lobotomy patient apoplectic. Apoplectic!" he shouted, then leaned even closer and went on with great intensity. "Anyway, I admit it, Ethan and I spent a lovely weekend in Vermont. Like the whores of Babylon, we were. But the little jerk couldn't keep his mouth shut. Word got out. Oh, don't say it. Of course, it was my fault. I know that you fool. Even so, did Ethan have to blab? Long story short, Richard found out. He left me and now…" King gestured helplessly to the video. "The big idiot is on *Love Me or Leave Me*, the story of three generations of Swedish Meatpackers and their daughters. Atrocious!"

Again, King tried to stand. Again, Ben pulled him down to the seat.

"I need another drink," King said. He dabbed his eyes. "That's what I need."

"You've had enough," Ben said, waving away the Steward.

"Then give me a goddamned Kleenex."

Ben found an unused napkin, and King noisily blew his nose.

"Another!"

This time when he dabbed his eyes, Ben saw actual tears, more than one.

"Congratulations," King said. "You've seen an old man cry."

He blew his nose again. Then he looked back to the video screen and shook his head. Though Ben couldn't hear the words, he could see Richard, a handsome, robust man in his late sixties, saying a line. Without even being able to hear, Ben could tell the material was beneath him. Richard had a dignity and a bearing that cried out for the stage.

"Look at him," King said, more composed.

"Does he do theater anymore?"

"Some stuff in LA but mostly TV. Commercials, too. Apparently, he's a spokesman for some sort of Foot Fungus. The medicine you smear on it."

"I missed that one," Ben said. "But no theater...in New York?"

King shrugged. "If he has, I wouldn't know it. But I tell you, the man is brilliant. Any show would be lucky to have him."

"Any show?"

"Yes, any show."

Ben couldn't resist. "He'd make a hell of a Judge Barkle."

If Ben expected that comment to trigger another rant, he was wrong. Instead, the old man dabbed his eyes and then nodded briskly.

"He would, wouldn't he?" Then he forced a sad smile. "Couldn't you see him with a caramel apple attached to his face?"

"I could."

"But don't you dare suggest it to Everett Walker," King went on. "As you just saw by my sad little display, I still miss the big sell-out. If I saw him again, I might kill him."

"I hear you."

"I don't plan to finish my life as a murderer," King groused.

"I understand."

"Good." King yawned deeply. "I need to sleep this off. Remind me not to drink so much on the return flight."

"I will."

"OK, then, thanks for listening." King yawned again. "Thank the rest of first class, too. I guess I put on quite a show… quite a show."

King dozed off, first fitfully, then deeply, leaving Ben awake. Carefully, he reached over and turned off King's video console. Then to his surprise, he found himself humming a familiar tune.

With a caramel apple stuck upon my face!

Ben smiled. Richard Sinclair would be inspired casting. Ben could see him perfectly capturing Judge Nathaniel Barkle's singular apple-related distress. Too bad it could never work. For starters, King would never allow it. And who knew if Richard Sinclair would even be interested in being in a musical at all, especially one written by his ex-lover?

"Oh, well," Ben thought.

Stuck Upon My Face! My Face!

He hummed the tune again, now keeping beat by the gentle rhythm of King's snores. Then Ben leaned across and pressed the "recline" button on the old man's chair so he could stretch out. Stretching out himself, he allowed himself a final wistful hope that the workshop would be a success, that King would sober up and behave, that Everett Walker's direction wouldn't be any weirder than the material warranted.

"Please," he whispered. "Make it good."

With that, Ben closed his eyes and went back to sleep.

12

That's why it's plain to tell
You want my pieces of Sanabelle.
You're loving my boots, you're digging my gel.
You want pieces – pretty pieces – of Sanabelle!

Life was sometimes wonderfully strange. In the blink of a week, Ben found himself with an arm around Mo's waist in the lavish mansion of international rock star Sir Eric Sanabelle. A friend of Everett Walker, Sanabelle had attended the workshop then spontaneously offered his place for a make-shift cast party, a gathering that quickly devolved into a drunken sing-along. Now the great Sanabelle himself was at the piano. Dressed in gold pants and a silver shirt, he was leading the crowd in a medley of his best-known songs.

"This is wild," Mo whispered. "Is Eric Sanabelle really playing piano for us?"

Ben nodded. At that moment, the icon was banging out a florid solo from "Pieces of Sanabelle," eight bars of tuneful rock that anyone in their mid-twenties to early forties would be certain to recognize.

"If not, it's someone who looks a hell of a lot like him who can sure pound the keys."

"Hey," someone from the crowd yelled. "Can you play something from *Dalmatians*?"

"Of course," Sanabelle replied, his accent decidedly

cockney.

Ben smiled.

"What?" Mo asked.

"Get ready to hear a misadventure in rhymes."

"Oh, you mean creature and sheet fur?" she asked.

Ben laughed. He couldn't wait to report back to his friends at the AMI workshop. "That and more."

Mo smiled and took a healthy drink, leaving a lipstick mark on the glass. Ben gave her a kiss.

"I'm glad you're here."

"I'm glad you're glad," Mo said. "The show was really good, by the way."

"Really? So was your manuscript."

"You said."

"I liked when the African warlords take on the goblins."

Mo laughed. "A bit different than a dead horse and divorce."

"True," Ben said. "You're versatile."

"You, too," Mo said. "I can't wait for a full production with sets so I can see these pies roller-skate for real."

Ben laughed. "Me, too."

He kissed her again, wishing they had had more time to see each other. Apparently, Mo was thinking the same thing.

"Too bad we only had time for one cup of coffee before this."

"I know," Ben said. "Once rehearsals started, things were crazy. Everett Walker is strange as hell, but he doesn't fool around."

"Rewrites?"

"On the rewrites, which also had rewrites. The guy practically critiqued the punctuation. Anyway, we're here now, right?"

Ben realized there was no one he'd rather be with. Suddenly, he found Mo's short hair and lipstick, jeans, and black boots the most attractive stylistic choice he had ever seen. With another quick kiss, the couple turned back to the piano and joined the final chorus of the infamous "White Fur, Black Spots" from *Dalmatians*:

Tell me, baby, do you have the hots
For white fur, honey
With black spots!

Just hold my paws
Connect my dots
On my white fur, honey
With black spots!

As Sir Sanabelle nodded from the keys, acknowledging compliments and applause, Horatio King moved to Ben's side. Excepting Ben's quick meet-up with Mo the first day in town, the two collaborators had been on best behavior all week – no drinking, no dating, just hard work – but now, with the workshop a success, all bets were off. While Ben was drinking with Mo, King had been enjoying several adult beverages himself.

"I see you're having some fun," King said, negotiating the party with his cane.

"We are," Ben said.

"Me, too." King leaned close. "Too bad this music is so dreadful."

Ben whispered back. "Don't tell that to my cousin. She's a big fan. By the way, this is Mo."

"Hi, Mr. King."

King took Mo's hand. To Ben's surprise, the old man gave it a kiss.

"I've been waiting for this social cretin to finally introduce us, my dear."

"A pleasure."

"No, it's all mine."

"I'm a big fan. I love *Twice Upon a Time*, in particular."

King smiled. "Please don't tell me that you played Felicia back in college with a limp."

Mo looked confused. "No, why?"

King winked at Ben. "Nothing. Anyway, you like my work, and I am flattered. You're the girl with the raccoon, correct?"

Thankful for the dim lighting, Ben felt himself turning red.

"He's the only person I told. He has a habit of saying everything."

"Relax, it's okay," Mo said. "Yeah, a raccoon. Ben's idea of romance."

"Well, you should be okay here," King said. "What are the odds of another nocturnal beast interrupting you in London?"

Mo gave Ben's hand a drunken squeeze. "We'll be careful."

"You better be," King said. "This boy is what we call a serial monogamist."

"Um, not true," Ben said, trying to keep it light.

"Okay then," King said, turning to Mo. "I'll put it this way. Ben here thinks he wants to be in love, but he's just too damned young. I guess I do talk too much. Should keep my big yap shut."

"Yeah," Ben said. Then he smiled. "You know, I was thinking…"

"What?" King asked.

Ben's smile turned into a full-fledged grin. "How good Richard Sinclair would be as Judge Barkle. I mean, if the show moves to New York."

King forced back a smile. "Shut the fuck up about Richard, will you?"

"Stop calling me a serial monogamist."

King shrugged. "All right, deal." Then he looked to Mo. "Forget what I said about Ben. He's been thinking about you non-stop."

Mo laughed. "Got it."

"I actually have," Ben admitted.

"Anyway, this isn't about our respective love lives," King said, "it's about the show. We have some things to discuss, of course – mostly how in God's name we're going to stage the skating apple pies."

"That's what I wondered," Mo said.

"Smart girl," King said. "But that'll be our designer's problem, I suppose. Of course, there are lots of trims and cuts." He put a hand on Ben's shoulder. "But all in all, we did a lot of good work in a short time. Not a bad first run, kid."

In truth, Ben had been so thrilled by the workshop that he hadn't taken notes. He was aware that it ran too long, but cutting was always easy, wasn't it? More important was the audience's incessant laughter throughout the whole show. On a basic level, the musical worked, there was no doubt about it. The crowd had been entertained.

Then King sidled closer, putting an arm on Ben's shoulder for support.

"Look over there," he said with a nod. "Across the room."

Ben glanced over his shoulder to where Everett Walker was chatting with a middle-aged woman with a smile several teeth too large for her face.

"Remember when you asked me about moving this show to

New York?" King went on.

"Uh, yes. Of course."

"Well, I told you that Everett would help us with British investors. That lady over there is Maria Feltenstein. She's practically salivating to write a check."

"How can you tell?" Mo asked.

"Her eyes – they're glittering like a stoned monkey."

Mo laughed. "You've seen a stoned monkey before?"

"No, but I can imagine."

Stoned monkey or not, Everett Walker began to cut through the crowd, leading Maria in their direction.

"Get ready to be charming," King said. "This lady is good for half a mil."

"Hello," Walker called above the sound of the singers on the piano. They were now belting out another of Sanabelle's famous tunes, "Deep Maroon on Orange Ice."

"Glad to have caught you both together."

Embarrassed that he had dropped the ball with King, Ben introduced Mo immediately.

"Ah, I saw you in the audience," Walker said. "Nice to meet you. We're all big fans of Ben."

Ben fought a blush. "Thanks."

"That's good," Mo said. "I guess I'm a fan, too."

Ben couldn't resist. "A big one?"

"Not sure yet. Give me a couple of hours."

King laughed. "I like this lady, Ben. As I said, I can see you with a nice Catholic."

"I'm Presbyterian," Mo said.

King shrugged. "That, too."

"If we're done talking religion," Walker said. "I'd like you all to meet someone. One of Britain's biggest producers, Maria

Feltenstein."

Handshakes all around.

"To be honest, I thought I was going to hate it," Maria said once the introductions were complete. "But it was simply lovely. All those wild desserts. I especially liked the pie that spoke in Swahili."

"Oh, good," King said. "It's all from Ben's very funny book."

"So I hear," Maria said. "I just ordered a copy. And I love Sylvester Sweet's dessert – the one he wins with every year. What is it again?"

"A double-chocolate-fudge-raspberry-coconut-lime swirl," Ben said.

"Sounds delicious," Maria said.

"Actually, it sounds disgusting," King said, "but what do I know?"

"Anyway, Maria is very interested in coming aboard," Everett said.

She flashed her too-large-for-her-face smile. "Like I said, I didn't expect to be having this conversation. But your workshop won me over. I've been looking to invest in something with a positive message, something I can bring my kids to. I'm going home to write a nice little check, just as soon as you tell me who is going to be your lead producer and I get the appropriate paperwork."

King bowed. "Thank you kindly. We hope to have word on that before we leave town."

"Are you hoping for Jeremy Higgins?"

"Good God no," King said. "He's putting his money into horses now, very slow ones, unfortunately."

"How about Patricia Hader?"

135

"She's a bright lady," Walker said. "But she's a Brit. I think we need someone American who understands the ins and out of Broadway."

"I know who'd be perfect," Maria said. "Theo Ribaldi."

"Dead," Horatio replied.

Maria looked startled. "I had lunch with him last month."

"He's technically living, I suppose," King said. "But since he pulled the plug on *Black Hawk Down,* he's dead to me."

Ben remembered. Theo Ribaldi was the lead producer of King's most notorious flop.

"You think he should've kept it running?" Ben asked.

"More than two days?" King said. "Hell yes! There were good things about that show. We could've built an audience."

Walker clapped King on the back. "Don't get caught up in the past, Horatio. *Black Hawk* was admirably ambitious."

"More than ambitious," King snapped. "It had depth. Power!"

Walker grinned. "Which might have come out more clearly had you asked me to direct."

King's eyes went wide. "Do you forget? You were working at the National then, doing that ballet set on the eve of the Louisiana Purchase."

Walker nodded. "That I was."

"But back to our apple pies," King said. He turned to Walker. "I suppose you've figured out how you're going to get them to roller-skate?"

"Oh, we'll work that out. I'm thinking of a giant puppet or something using wires. What I'm more worried about is the second act."

"Oh?" King asked.

Walker scratched his ample chin. "The first act gets by on

136

charm but I think we need to get a bit moodier as the play goes on, maybe a song where Applefeller is feeling completely taken in by the dark side of dessert."

"The dark side of dessert...?" Ben began.

"No, that could be interesting, Ben," King said. "An aria where Applefeller questions everything."

"Right," Walker said then rubbed Ben's shoulder. "All to be discussed. We'll work it out. And by the way, guys. I've been thinking. Should we move to New York, I'd like to bring on Sven Nordgren as a dramaturg."

"Sven Nordgren?" Ben said. His voice caught in his throat. "The playwright?"

"That's right," Walker said. "And a damned fine one."

"I'm sure," Ben said. "But his stuff is really dark, right? He won an Oliver Award for a tragedy about Napoleon."

"Actually, it was Genghis Khan, the early years," King said.

"Even worse," Ben said.

King turned to Walker. "Ben has a point. Do you think Sven is right for our piece?"

Walker nodded. "Oh, yes. I think someone with a darker vision could be of great benefit."

"But he's a writer," Ben repeated.

Walker winked at King. "Our boy genius has to learn to relax, doesn't he?" Walker rubbed Ben's shoulder again. "Sven will be our dramaturg – all he'll do is suggest cuts and changes. He won't write a word, promise."

"And if Ben and I don't like his suggestions?" King asked. "I'm sure as hell not going to change our script because some well-awarded Norwegian tells us to."

Walker's eyes went wide, obviously delighted at the anxiety he had stirred up. "Look at the both of you. So nervous! No, no, no. Sven will just be here to advise, all right? If you don't like something he suggests, don't do it. You'll see. Everything is going to be fine. Better than fine. With a little work, we'll have a big fat hit."

"That's how I like them," Maria Feltenstein said. "Big and fat."

With that, Walker began to expand upon his design concept for the show which entailed filling the lobby with wacky dessert booths so the audience felt as though it was entering the contest itself. Ben was half listening, still concerned about Nordgren when Mo leaned close.

"You look tense."

"A little."

"Want to get out of here?"

"Leave the party?"

Mo kissed him on the cheek and whispered in his ear. "Wanna explore? I hear there are thirty rooms."

Ben liked the idea. He also wasn't stupid enough not to realize what he thought Mo was suggesting.

"Will Sir Sanabelle be okay with that?"

Mo shrugged and looked toward the piano where the rock star turned musical theater composer had moved on from his own oeuvre to a stirring rendition of "Brandy, You're a Fine Girl." "He's not going to notice anyway, right?"

Ben didn't have to be told twice. As Walker continued to wax poetic, now about the set, ("It's going to be made of actual desserts. You'll see!"), the couple drained their drinks and were soon walking up a sweeping stairway, the walls lined with posters from Sanabelle's various concert tours as well as a litany of framed Platinum records and Album covers.

"Which way?" Ben asked.

Mo shrugged and pointed up. "Another flight?"

"Hey," Ben said as they climbed. "You never told me exactly what you liked best about the show."

"Are we talking about the show now?" Mo asked. She gave Ben a long kiss. "I thought we were looking for a room."

Ben laughed. Was he really being that self-absorbed about his career? "We are. Sorry, yes, of course. But…"

His voice trailed off.

"But what?" Mo laughed. "You look nervous."

"About Everett Walker," Ben said. "I don't see why we need a moodier song. You really liked it the way it is, didn't you?"

Mo took Ben's hands in hers. "The show is charming."

"*Charming*? Doesn't sound like a compliment when you say it like that."

"Say it like what?"

"Like you said it."

"Charming is a good thing. The show doesn't try to be anything it's not."

"Tell that to Everett Walker," Ben said.

Mo shrugged. "He's supposed to be a weird genius, right? Maybe the show needs some darkness mixed with the charm. Some bitter topping for the dessert."

"Maybe," Ben said. "But Jesus!" He laughed. "Did you hear him? He wants to bring on a playwright whose claim to fame is writing about one of history's most prolific murderers."

Mo laughed. "That's true, I guess."

Ben shook his head. "This could be a disaster."

"A disaster?" Mo patted his cheek. "Last I looked, your novel is being turned into a musical with Horatio King. Is that a disaster?"

"No, I guess not." Ben shook himself then kissed Mo again.

"Things aren't all bad."

Mo pointed up the stairs to a doorway. "I bet that's a bedroom. I bet the door locks."

"Ah, ha," Ben said. "How convenient. Do we dare?"

"Worried about gophers? Or groundhogs this time?"

"Actually, I was hoping for groundhogs."

Mo took his hand. "Let's see."

They took the stairs two at a time. Though the first room was a study – a large one with a fireplace – the second they checked was a guest room with a bureau, a flat-screen TV, a red upright piano, and most importantly, a queen-sized bed.

"Ha, ha," Mo said. "Jackpot."

She kissed his lips, then his neck. Ben kicked the door closed, locked it with one hand, then fell with Mo to the bed.

"You know what?" he said.

"What?"

"I like you."

Ben surprised himself even as the words came out of his mouth.

"I like you, too," Mo said. She laughed. "Even though you're a serial monogamist."

Ben began to object.

"Don't deny it. Even your own collaborator knows it."

"I don't even know what that really means," Ben said. "But whatever it is, I'm trying to grow out of it. Doesn't that count for anything?"

"Yeah, a little."

Mo kissed him again on the lips. Ben kissed her back but then paused, overcome with a new feeling, one he hadn't expected. He felt slightly hesitant to sleep with someone – because he liked her too much.

"What's wrong?"

Ben forced a smile. "Would you laugh if I said I don't want to get hurt?"

Mo smiled. "Get hurt?"

"Yeah."

Mo kissed him again, extra gently this time. "Don't worry. This isn't going to hurt at all."

13

King craned his neck and laughed.

"Is it really that funny?" Ben asked.

The collaborators were on the plane home, again side by side, again first class. King had pried and nudged until Ben had revealed what had happened. Though Ben had been looking for sympathetic counsel, King had not risen to the occasion.

"So let me get this straight," the old man said. "You snuck up to the third floor of Sanabelle's mansion. For a little inebriated early evening recreation."

"You could call it that."

"I don't blame you. That Mo is a nice young lady. Liked her."

"Me, too."

King leaned closer and took another swig of his requisite scotch, a prop, Ben was finding, on any flight.

"I thought you looked a little bit sheepish when you came back downstairs. When push came to shove, there was no shove?"

Ben shuddered. That wasn't the way he would have put it. But yes. Something about the surroundings – the strange room, the noise from the party below, maybe even the glare from the red upright – had gotten in his way.

"You might say that," Ben said. "I couldn't…I mean…you know…"

King sighed. For a split second, Ben was worried that King

was going to announce it to the rest of the first class.

"Relax," King said. "You're fine."

"I am?"

"Sure."

"It's happened to you?"

King blinked. "You mean it's never happened to you?"

Ben shook his head. "Actually, no."

King's eyes went wide then he laughed. "Welcome to adulthood, kid." He took another drink. "And get used to it. As you get older, this will happen more and more. Besides, I think I know what went wrong."

"Really? What?"

"Or should I say who?"

"Who?"

King leaned closer. "Sven Nordgren."

"Sven Nordgren?" Ben said. "What does he have to do with it?"

King waved a finger. "I saw the look in your eye when Everett suggested that he come on board. The abject fear. The blind panic that comes when a dramaturg arrives on the scene."

"Yeah, maybe," Ben said. "But so panicked that I couldn't you know...?"

"We just had a very successful workshop," King went on. "Then our director tells us he's bringing on a dramaturg who happens to be a well-regarded writer. Hell, I was surprised, too. Face it: you wanted to concentrate on your lady but were preoccupied."

Ben had to admit it. He had been thinking about Sven Nordgren more than he cared to admit.

"Felled by a Norwegian playwright," King said with a chuckle. "Check and mate. But don't look so depressed. It's happened to me, too."

"Oh, really?" Ben said. "You've thought about Sven Nordgren during... you know?"

King scowled. "God, no. But when I was working on *Twice Upon a Time,* I had a beautiful boyfriend. His nickname was "the Thunk," of all things. His physique had a physique if you know what I mean. All muscle. I couldn't get interested in sex from the first preview through opening night. Too much at stake."

Ben nodded. Mo had even suspected as much, eventually apologizing for dragging him upstairs on a night when he had so much on his mind.

Suddenly, King was giggling.

"What?" Ben asked.

"You have to admit that it's pretty funny. First, a raccoon, then a playwright."

Ben had to laugh. "Yeah, I suppose."

"Don't you worry," King said, patting Ben's hand. "You'll have your chance. That girl likes you."

"I like her, too."

Ben couldn't quite believe how forcefully the words came out. King raised an eyebrow and pulled gently on his beard.

"Well, well, well. Could it be? Another reason your performance might have been hindered, my boy. Like I said, you've never been in love."

As usual when talking to King, Ben found himself feeling vaguely pissed off. It was time to set the record straight.

"I told my college girlfriend I loved her senior year."

"Ah, yes. The famous Gretchen."

"Right."

"How many times did you tell her?"

"Does it matter?"

"Of course, it matters!"

Ben paused. "To be honest…once."

"Once?" King guffawed. "That's nothing, kid. I bet you whispered it, too, so she could barely hear."

"Hell, no!" Now it was Ben's turn to shout in First Class. He brought his voice down to a sharp whisper. "I said it full out on the campus green, okay? We have a deal where we're going to marry when we're forty-three and a half. So don't say I've never been in love."

King looked at Ben as though he was insane. "You have a deal?"

"Yeah."

King shook his head. "You've never been in love. If you were, you wouldn't wait until your forties to seal it."

It was all Ben could do not to slap King. Or at least give his beard a sharp yank.

"Oh, don't look so sulky," King said with a laugh. "You know I'm right. Gretchen sounds like a nice girl from Vermont. Do you really see yourself in a log cabin slathering her with maple syrup for the next eighty years? No, Mo is more up your alley. A nice young lady, a writer. A lipstick-wearing city girl. She's who you should be with, and it scares you."

"She doesn't scare me."

"Of course she does. You only saw her twice the whole time we were in the country."

Ben couldn't deny that.

"You told me not to date. We were busy."

"Not that busy."

"She's in London now anyway."

"So what? Three more months, right? It'll fly-by"

"Four."

"Okay, four. But distance can be a good thing. Write her emails. Call her occasionally. Let the anticipation build. Love is best when simmered."

"Since when are you such an expert?"

King sighed. "I'm not, you fool. But I'm old enough to know that opportunities like Mo Ryan, children's author, do not come around every day. And don't you dare bring up Richard Sinclair again. I already fucked that up. I'm trying to keep the same thing from happening to you."

Ben nodded. He saw that King, in his own strange way, was trying to be supportive.

"Just think," King said. "If you finally get together, the raccoon and Eric Sanabelle will make a hell of a story."

"I suppose," Ben said. He paused. "You really think Sven Nordgren won't be a problem?"

"With your sex life?"

"No, no – with the show."

King drained his glass. "Let's not forget something, Ben. I'm Horatio King, right?"

"Right."

The old man leaned close again. "How many Tonys do I have?"

"Eight?"

"And a few Grammys as well, along with an Oscar for that crap song I wrote for that shit movie. Now how about our friend Sven?"

"I don't know," Ben said. "He has an Olivier."

"Correct," King said. "One lousy Olivier! He's done close to nothing."

"Nothing?"

"Compared to me?"

"Well, that's true."

"Damn right, it's true. So if Mr. Nordgren suggests something we don't like, we tell him to piss off. No one fucks with me."

Ben felt notably relieved. The tension he had felt since the end of the workshop began to dissipate. He suddenly wished that Mo was there right then for another chance.

"Now," King went on. "Try not to have a seizure, but I do think the idea of a darker song in Act Two isn't bad."

Ben blinked. "Wait. You actually liked that idea?"

"It's worth trying," King said. "Give the show a little more weight. Why don't you work on a lyric while I get quietly drunk."

Ben smiled. "As long as you're quiet."

"What?" King said with a smile. "You didn't appreciate my mental breakdown on the way over? Oh, but the rest of first class probably loved it. What a story they got to tell their friends. Saw a famous composer lose his shit over the Atlantic. Ah, relax." King shook his glass. "This is only my third, and it's going to be my last. You don't have to worry this time. I'll be a good boy." King yawned. "But do think a bit about that lyric."

"Okay, but what should it be about?"

"Well, Applefeller is awfully driven by his desire to win the Silver Spoon, isn't he?"

"Right."

"Maybe he feels it's overwhelming him. Maybe the force of the Spoon is so strong he feels like it's cluttering his mind, making him behave in ways he doesn't approve. What do you think?"

Ben nodded. "I think I see it. But then he wins at the end with his own dessert and is redeemed."

"Precisely." King yawned. "Call it something like

147

'Bittersweet' or "Dark Chocolate.' Whatever. And while we're at it, I do think Sylvester Sweet needs a song in Act Two, something fun and villainous. So we can see his history."

With those thoughts, King finished his drink.

"You work. I'll rest. By the way, another piece of good news."

"What?"

"Before we left, Everett thought of a person to be the lead producer of our show. A young gal named Michelle Marks. Raised money for about ten smaller productions. Now she's champing at the bit to step into the spotlight."

"Great," Ben said. He had vaguely heard of her – something about a musical she had developed based on the Wright Brothers' forgotten half-sister. "Is she interested?"

"Everett sent her an email last night and she responded right away. Very enthusiastic." King smiled. "She said something about bringing in additional investors through the internet. I think she's a smart one."

Ben nodded. "Great. Whatever works. What do you think the show will cost?"

King shrugged. "At today's prices? Ten million?"

Ben shuddered. "My God. That's insane."

"Welcome to the big leagues, son. But raising the money isn't our problem, thank God. Just the writing. Work on that lyric, won't you?"

With that, King stretched out and closed his eyes. For his part, Ben reached dutifully for his computer. Another benefit of First Class: the internet worked. Yes, he would work on a lyric, of course, he would. But first things first: he would type a short email to Mo.

Hey – writing this over the Atlantic. First Class. Feeling a bit strange about Eric Sanabelle and his guest room. But I hope we can keep in touch. I want to read more of your book. Please send me the pages when you have them. And I'll really look forward to seeing you back in New York in four months."

Ben re-read the note. Not inspired, but it would have to do. He was about to press send when he heard the "bring" of an incoming message. To his surprise, it was from Mo. Eagerly, but a bit nervously, Ben opened it.

Hi,

Thanks for the wonderful time at Eric Sanabelle's humble abode. I love spending time with you, Ben...but I do feel bad about something. I'm afraid that I wasn't totally honest. I didn't mean for it to happen this way, believe me, but for the past two months, I've been involved with an ex who is now living in London, a guy named Nate, a lawyer.

Like I said, I feel pretty awful about it, but after our innocent cup of coffee the first afternoon you arrived, I assumed that the night of your reading would be more of the same: more innocence. But then I got swept up in the thrill of the night... swept away by you, too (and too much to drink).

Suffice it to say, I'm confused. I'm here in London, and so is Nate. You're headed back to New York. Even so, I do care about you, Ben, raccoons and all. I wish you great luck on your show and look forward to staying in touch... as writing buddies for the time being. What do you think?

Again, sorry for any deception.

Love, Mo

Ben read the email twice, more disappointed than he would have expected. He knew that he and Mo had only been on two real dates, both marked by aborted sexual encounters. Even so, he felt the loss. For a second, he thought of telling Horatio King. But the old man was sound asleep, snoring lightly. Besides, there was always the chance that King would merely laugh – or worse, force his way into the cockpit and announce Ben's predicament over the loudspeaker.

He pressed "delete" on his own email, a message that suddenly felt as though it had been written a lifetime ago. Yes, the raccoon and Sven Nordgren would have made a nice story. But now they made another story, one of missed opportunities.

"Shit," Ben said.

The hell with Mo, he thought. He had never really liked her. Ben knew it was a lie, of course, but it made him feel temporarily better. Still, he couldn't talk himself out of a nagging disappointment. Even after downing a drink; even after trying his hand (unsuccessfully) at the new lyric, "Dark Chocolate," Ben still felt as though he had blown it. With no other way to escape the letdown, Ben reclined his seat, aiming to shoot for a few hours of uneasy sleep. It was one thing to be single, ostensibly carefree. That had its moments, after all, benefits that sometimes outweighed the inherent loneliness. But to be single and side-swiped by regret? That was no fun.

14

Most musicals take years to develop, workshops that lead to more workshops that lead to readings before finally – maybe – garnering a production at a regional theater, perhaps in Santa Barbara or Oklahoma City. Fueled by the success of the London Workshop, *Just Desserts* took off on a uniquely speedy trajectory. While most shows take months or years to raise capital, Michelle Marks and her producing team raised the necessary funds in less than two weeks, opening up the kitty to first-time investors through a website she named GODESSERT.COM.

"I guess people still have faith in the old man, after all," King told Ben the day the show was capitalized. "Watch if we don't bring in a big hit."

"That's great," Ben said. "But you don't think we're bringing it in too fast?"

"Too fast?" King shook his head. "*Black Hawk Down* was killed by too many workshops, the life clean sucked out of it. No, *Just Desserts* will be old school. The way they did it in the 30s. The workshop went like gangbusters so now we put on an actual show, eh? Sound good?"

It sounded great. But there was still another major hurdle to clear before Ben could fantasize about how the show might be received: finding the right venue. Typically, a producer with a new musical had no choice but to get in line and hope for other shows to close. Here Horatio King's mammoth reputation saved the day: now that the workshop had been a hit, the prospect of housing the first musical by the great master in over a decade pushed *Just Desserts* to the front of the queue. When a well-reviewed but poorly attended play based on Tim O'Brien's *The Things We Carried* closed, Michelle Marks was able to retain the theater after a day's negotiation.

And so three mere weeks after King and Ben returned from England, the press had the news. After a stunningly successful London workshop, *Just Desserts* would start previews at the *Imperial* in two months on April 10th, then open on April 26th, a day before the end of the theater season, just in time to be considered for that year's Tony Awards.

It was risky, heady stuff. Ben dealt with the stress by burying himself in work. While he struck pay dirt quickly with a new humorous song for Sylvester Sweet, "The King of Dessert," the darker lyric for Applefeller, the "cry of despair" (in Walker's words) that would lend the show deeper meaning, was giving him fits. Lines were written and discarded. Frustrated, one morning at two, Ben suggested a possible way forward: bringing the best draft of what he had to the AMI workshop.

"The workshop?" King spat. "Ethan Hancock and his band of idiots?"

"So," Ben asked with a smile. "Is that a no?"

King mouthed the word: "no."

Still, Ben kept working.

"So how's this?" he asked Harrison one afternoon. The roommates were relaxing in the apartment, Ben in the living room area, and Harrison making a pot of coffee in the erstwhile rat corral. "*I've discovered my life has gone to shit/When I'm living a sin of dark chocolate?*"

"Well, the rhyme works," Harrison said. "Shit and

chocolate."

"But…?" Ben asked.

Harrison shrugged. "Isn't this a family show?"

"Sure," Ben said. "But this is Applefeller's breakdown."

"But Dark Chocolate and shit?" Harrison said. "That's pretty on the nose, isn't it?"

"On the nose?"

"You can do better."

Ben shook his head but pressed delete, erasing the offending line.

"There, gone. Happy?"

"Very."

Ben sighed. Despite the positive trajectory of the show, it had been a tough couple of weeks emotionally. He had finally responded to Mo, writing a friendly email communicating that while he was disappointed, he understood about Nate, and yes, they would remain writing buddies.

"Wow," Harrison had said when he had read the note before Ben had sent it. "That's mature as hell."

Maybe so but, maturity aside, Ben felt lonely. To make matters worse, Harrison was gearing up to move in with Justin, news he had broken a day after Ben's return. Then one night, late, cruising Instagram, Ben came upon a picture of Mo and a good-looking guy, undoubtedly Nate. Moreover, the post included a series of shots, a night out, that included the seemingly happy couple at the theater, walking by the Thames, then seated at a bistro in front of their main course, a nice-looking risotto.

"Shit," Ben muttered.

After pacing his apartment for a hot minute, Ben complained to Justin. Still agitated, he moved to his go-to therapy: a quick call to Gretchen. (In keeping with their open friendship, she was up to date on all things "Mo," including the failure in Eric Sanabelle's mansion). But when Ben got Gretchen's voicemail, it seemed too pitiful to admit even to a best friend how a single Instagram post had brought him to his knees. Instead, he left an innocuous message and then tortured himself anew, glancing once again at the infamous pictures.

With Mo in London, Gretchen in Vermont, and Harrison packing to move, Ben at least had Horatio King to keep him occupied. The old man was clearly tired, occasionally showing his years, but like an aging athlete, he was capable of great bursts of energy. As auditions grew closer, Everett Walker announced that he was coming to New York for good (or through the opening anyway) to oversee all the elements of the production. By that time, Ben had all but forgotten about the looming threat of Sven Nordgren. To the extent he thought of the dramaturg's notes at all, he assumed that his comments were so minor that Everett Walker hadn't deemed them worth passing along. But a month to the day after returning from England, Ben pushed through King's front door to find a surprise: Everett Walker slouching by the mantle.

"There he is," Walker called. "The boy genius."

Ben forced a grin.

"Yep," he said. "Here I am."

"Good to see you," King called from the sofa. "You'd better come on in and take a seat."

Ben didn't like the sound of that. Had some of the show's funding fallen through? Worse, had they lost the theater? Over the past week, King had been a never-ending vessel of enthusiasm and irascible good spirits. Now he sounded vaguely pissed off.

"Got an email," Walker called.

"An email?" Ben said, trying to figure out what that could mean.

"Relax," Walker said. "Everything's OK."

Entering the living room, Ben noticed Walker holding a folded piece of paper, clearly a printout of some sort. Then he put it together.

"Oh," he said. "Sven Nordgren?"

"He makes some rather interesting points," Walker said.

"Interesting points?" Ben said. Again, that didn't sound good. "But he basically liked it, right?"

"Like isn't really the right word," King grunted.

More than vaguely pissed off. Seething.

"He didn't hate it, did he?" Ben asked with a laugh.

Walker chuckled. "Oh, no. He thinks it's all going to be wonderful."

Now Ben was seriously worried.

"Going to be wonderful?"

King came out with it. "After we completely rewrite the fucking thing."

Ben felt his heart begin to race. "What?"

"Relax, you two," Walker said. "The piece just needs a little shading."

"Shading?" King said. "Why don't you read his letter to Ben and see what he thinks?" He turned to Ben. "You'd better sit for this."

Nervously, Ben did as he was told. It appeared to him that King looked a bit pale. Was the old man merely mildly annoyed or abjectly furious? Or maybe just hurt? Tellingly, he stroked Juniper, seemingly wanting the dog's comfort.

"All right then," Walker said. "Shall we begin?"

"Yes," King said. "Slit our throats."

"Come now, Horatio. It's not that bad."

"Read!"

Walker cleared his throat.

"Dear Mr. King and Mr. Willis," he began. "Sorry for the delay, but I am writing you today from a Writer's Colony in Iceland, where I am assiduously at work on my new play, *Genghis: The Sensitive Years*."

King shot Ben a glance. "That sounds like a winner."

"Since when was Genghis Khan sensitive?" Ben asked.

"Since he slaughtered half a continent."

Walker continued. "Let me start by saying what an honor it is to have been asked to evaluate your play for Broadway. Mr. King: I am one of your biggest fans. Mr. Willis: I am a new comer to your work but already an admirer."

"That doesn't sound so bad," Ben said.

He allowed himself a shiver of relief. Perhaps Sven Nordgren would be much ado about nothing?

"Not yet anyway," King said. "But wait for it. Go!"

Walker cleared his throat.

"However," he read, turning back to the email. "I don't think that I would be doing great artists such as yourselves a service to blindly praise the work sent to me by our friend Everett Walker. That would be a betrayal of a friendship, would it not? It would also be a betrayal to myself as a theater artist. Resultantly, I have compiled some notes for you to bear in mind as you rewrite for Broadway. Cheers!"

"That doesn't sound good," Ben remarked.

"It isn't," King said. "Keep reading, Everett. Hold nothing back."

Now Walker read quickly – so quickly, in fact, that Ben couldn't take it all in. Mostly, it was a terrifying blur. While

Nordgren praised the show for its "originality" and "its moral commitment to telling a story that is old fashioned yet current" he took issue with the piece's "frivolous" tone. "Must musical theater be so facile?" he wrote. "Can't we have our cake and eat it, too?" Worse, he deemed Ben's lyrics "clever but lightweight" and penned "while the dialog has its witty moments, strange puns, and silly malapropisms, I'm wondering about its realism."

"The dialog is purposely heightened," Ben said. "Absurdist in parts but real enough."

"That's what I say," King said. "This man is a moron."

"Obviously, this is a light-hearted piece," Walker read, forging on. "But again, I return to my overriding point. Can't we be silly with depth? Silly for silly's sake is a rather unsatisfying meal. But silly with meat on the bones? That is a feast that will thrive in New York City's cold, harsh theater environment. As an experiment, I suggest dropping all the dialog as written and starting over."

Ben nearly fell out of his seat.

"Starting over? Is he serious?"

"I don't think Sven Nordgren has said a funny thing in his life," King said. "He's serious all right."

Ben blinked once, then blinked again, taking it in. "So he hates the lyrics and the dialog? What does he like?"

"Not the music," King intoned.

"Now, now," Walker said. "He doesn't say that."

"Oh, no?" King said. "Read on, MacDuff."

"Perhaps I better just stop," Walker said. "We've heard enough for now."

King leaned forward, menacingly. "Read the damned thing and read it now, or I'll get creative with my cane – on your body."

What else could Walker do?

"Now to the music. Oh, how I love the sound of Horatio King! His melodies have been the soothing balm to my soul on rainy days. His scores are at once rapturous and intelligent."

"So what's the problem?" Ben asked.

"It saddens me to say that this is neither," Walker continued. "Yes, there is a nice nostalgia for Rodgers & Hammerstein and the best of Lerner & Loewe but overall, this music holds a distant candle to those masters. None of what I call uniquely 'King' is present. Yes, there are catchy tunes. But is catchy enough when drama and depth are called for?"

"That brain-dead Norwegian dares to call me a second-rate Lerner and Loewe?" King cried, waving his cane. "I'll kill him."

"At least he didn't tell you to throw everything out," Ben said.

"The hell with him," King said. He looked to Walker. "Thanks for bringing your dramaturg aboard. Very helpful."

Walker forced a smile. "Perhaps he was a little bit harsh."

"A little harsh?" King roared. "He's a monster! Ben – let's hear your latest lyric. Recite the opening verse."

"Now?" Ben asked.

"Yes, now. The one sung by Sylvester Sweet. 'The King of Dessert.' Please!"

Ben did as he was told:

It all began the fateful morn,
The day that little me was born
A day that humankind will sanctify.

Emerging from my momma's womb,
I quickly crawled across the room
And made a double-split banana pie.

Then a hungry nurse, you see.
Ate the pie and diapered me
And wept into her skirt:
"Hail the newborn King of Dessert!
Hail the King of Dessert!"

The second Ben was done, King turned savagely to Walker.

"Now that, my friend, is fine lyric writing. It's amusing, well-rhymed, and unpretentious. It's a lyric that befits the tone of our show."

"I agree," Walker said.

"Ah, ha! You do?"

"Up to a point," Walker said.

"What do you mean?" King asked.

"That lyric presents the problem in stark relief," Walker said. "Yes, it is playful and funny. I'm sure your tune is charming, Horatio. But all the lyrics are like this. All the songs and the story are light-hearted."

"That's the fucking point," King said. "It's a light-hearted show whose deeper message about hard work and morality in today's dark times comes through subtly. That's what makes it great! That's what worked so well in the workshop."

"In the workshop, yes," Walker said. "But not in New York."

"What?" Ben said.

"New York, my boy," Walker repeated, turning to him. "I'm sorry to say, but today's audience needs more spices in the soup. Funny and light is good as far as it goes. But at one hundred and fifty bucks a seat, the work needs more depth."

"I get that we need a darker song for Act Two," King said.

"But aside from that, I'm lost. Tell me what the fuck you're talking about because I'm not precisely sure."

"I'm saying there can be more color," Walker said. "For instance, Sylvester Sweet – he's more than a mere villain, is he not? He's a strongman of the contest. The Eva Peron or even the Joseph Stalin!"

"Stalin?" King said. "You're out of your mind." He turned to Ben. "Are you hearing this? Our director is criminally insane."

Unperturbed, Walker went on. "And how about the other contestants in the contest? They're charming as far as they go, but why not make some of them more dangerous?"

"What?" King said. "You suggest we bring in a dessert chef from ISIS?"

Walker shrugged. "I'm just spit balling ideas here."

"They're terrible."

King stumbled to his mantle and picked up the famed Tony, *Lear*.

"I threw this at Ben, and I can throw it at you," the old man intoned, cocking his arm.

Juniper barked in anticipation. Ben was frozen. He hated what Walker was saying. On the other hand, could they really afford to have a falling out with their director right after announcing for Broadway and hiring an entire team of designers?

Walker backed out of the room. "Easy now, Horatio. That's an award, not a weapon."

King smiled, inching toward the famed director. "That's where you're wrong, Everett. When I received it, it was an award. Now I can do whatever the hell I want to with it. I could use it as a pigeon feeder or melt it down into a golden athletic supporter. Or throw it at your head! Now get out!"

"Really, Horatio!"

"I said, get the fuck out of my house. Come back when you're ready to talk sense."

Walker shook his head, smiling sadly.

"Don't you see, Horatio? This is what happened with *Black Hawk*."

King's eyes narrowed. "What?

"With *Black Hawk Down*."

"Yes, I'm well aware of the show."

"Are you? From what I saw on stage you had the beginnings of something very good, indeed, maybe even a masterpiece that could've survived and even thrived. But what did you do? You refused to take advice. At least that's what I heard around town. Don't you see that I'm trying to stop the same thing from happening here? We don't want a show that will close in a day. We want a hit! A hit with humor and whimsy but also depth and yes, little touches of despair."

"Touches of despair?" King said. His arm was still cocked, holding the Tony like a missile. "Like what?"

"Just what I said," Walker said. "Touches. Not a wholehearted rewrite."

"Sven Nordgren just said that Ben should rewrite every single line."

"Oh, the hell with Sven," Walker said. "He doesn't get it. But he does get the big picture, Horatio. He gets the shades of color this show needs to be a hit."

Ben still half expected King to let the Tony fly, putting Walker down for the count or at least taking out one of his kneecaps. Instead, the old man hesitated, seemingly thinking it all through. Then to Ben's surprise, King lowered his arm.

"Shades of color?"

"Yes, that's all!"

"What about my music?"

"Don't change a note. Sven is notoriously tone-deaf."

King took a shaky step forward. "This is who you hired as our dramaturg?"

"To evaluate the script, yes!" Walker turned to Ben. "And ignore what he said about rewriting every line. Sven's English is limited. He doesn't get your vernacular."

"But he still trashed the show," Ben said. "So what do we do next?"

"With your permission, gentlemen," Walker said, "we get to work. We go through the script line by line, thinking about how to make it more resonant. What do you say?"

King looked at Ben and sighed. Then he shuffled back toward the mantle. Though Ben still half expected him to wheel around and take a crack at Walker's head, he placed the Tony back on his shelf.

"More resonant, you say?"

"Right, that's all," Walker replied.

King looked to Ben. "We ought to be able to handle that."

Ben still wasn't precisely sure what that meant. To him, the show was perfectly resonant, amusing, and heartfelt. But what else could he say? If they could find ways to give the show added depth, wouldn't it be crazy not to try?

"Sure," Ben said. "Resonant."

"Nice," Walker said.

"I suppose you want to start right away then?" King said. "Before I even have a chance to take Juniper out for an afternoon piss."

Walker smiled. "We can wait for that. Besides, it'll give me time to write back to Sven."

"Sven?" Ben said. "What're you going to tell him?"

"Simple," Walker said. "That he's a braindead idiot. Now come! Walk that miserable mutt, then let's get to the script."

15

Over the next several weeks, Ben and King worked around the clock, living on take-out, cereal, and coffee, going through the script, tweaking lines to make them darker, bringing out fascistic parallels to Sylvester Sweet, and otherwise giving the show that patina of hipness and depth that Sven Nordgren said would make them a New York hit.

Most nights, Everett Walker would drop by after a day of meetings to check in on the team's progress. Ben soon discovered that if Horatio King was a hard worker, Everett Walker was a slave driver. Evaluating every line in the script meant every single line. Words were parsed for meaning, then parsed again. Lines were moved, cut, and then sometimes – only after a full dissection and analysis – reinstated. At the same time, King worked on the score, determined to keep it light but adding selective chords and phrases designed to surprise or perhaps even trouble the listener, lending the entire piece deeper shades of meaning.

And between rewrites were production meetings. There were discussions with the orchestrator (a light, cartoony sound), the lighting design team (a bright palate), and the scenic designer (those pesky roller-skating apple pies), not to mention meetings with lawyers, the costume designer, the music director, the music supervisor, the assistant director (Natalie French had been hired at Ben's suggestion), publicity department, the lighting designer, and the stage manager.

All of which lead to the big week of auditions. Though Ben thought better of suggesting Richard Sinclair to read for the role of Judge Nathaniel Barkle, literally hundreds of talented actors and actresses from around the country tried out, all hungry for a role in Horatio King's new show. In the end, King, Ben, Walker, and their casting team saw over three thousand actors and actresses and hired eighteen. The role of Applefeller was given to Joe Brady, a Broadway stalwart whose most recent role was Harold Hill in a well-received revival of *Music Man*. Applefeller's assistant, Samantha, went to Sylvia Johnson, a child actress known for a national Toys "R" Us ad. Sylvester Sweet was taken by film actor Philip Busterford.

Ben was pleased with the cast – the only exception being, ironically, Judge Barkle. Yes, Jack Shore was a perfectly acceptable actor but someone Ben wasn't sure possessed the requisite goofy charm to play a man with a caramel apple attached to his face. Still, Everett Walker wasn't worried. "I can get a performance out of anybody," he said. "Some actors just don't audition well." Reassured, Ben acquiesced. All in all, it was a superb cast – one to be excited about, the cast of a smash.

The first day of rehearsals was marked by a "meet and greet" where Everett Walker made a speech deeming *Just Desserts* "an important piece of musical theater, one that will take its place in the great canon of American work." Then the cast and crew went to work, days spent in a studio on 8th Avenue where Walker blocked the book scenes and staged the dances before moving to the theater. All the while, Ben was impressed, even slightly awed, by his director/choreographer's control of the proceedings. Yes, he had asked for plenty of changes, some of them unexpected, but how could a man so confident in his convictions be wrong? The show was different now, darker, moodier, that was certain.

But the hard work of the previous weeks had paid off. Having gone over every line and note, there was even less rewriting needed during rehearsals than Ben had anticipated – more evidence that his *Much Ado About Nothing* set in a barnyard aside, Everett Walker actually knew what he was doing. A good thing because before long it was time to move into the Imperial Theater itself for "tech," where the show was given over to the stage manager and technical crews to oversee lights and scenery. Working on *Just Desserts* to the point of overload, Ben hadn't realized just how desperate he was for a break. Thankfully, he had a pre-arranged get-away…

Three days before the first preview, the first week of April, found Ben maneuvering a rented Ford Hybrid up the Taconic Parkway, headed to the Middlebury Chamber of Commerce and Agrarian Society Bookfair.

Tech. Lights, Rehearsals. Broadway.

It wasn't until he crossed the state line into Vermont that Ben's mind finally began to clear a little. With Mo still in London with Nate (a week earlier, Ben had stumbled across another distressing picture of the couple), Ben had found himself thinking more and more about Gretchen, often reaching for the phone to say hello, simply to hear her voice. Slowly, through the morass of rewrites, meetings, and auditions, Ben began to realize something: when he and Gretchen had made their wedding pact, he had been a different, less serious person. Now he was on his way to Broadway, perhaps readier to settle down than he had previously given himself credit for. King had been right about one thing anyway: if Gretchen truly was the one, why was he waiting until he was forty-three and a half to close the deal?

And so as Ben drove into Middlebury, he found himself

envisioning an altogether more romantic rendezvous than he might have anticipated even a month or two earlier. He assumed that he and Gretchen would sleep together. He was spending the night at her home, after all. But maybe their time together could be more than good friendship and casual sex. Instead of idling in neutral, maybe they were both ready to push the relationship into overdrive. The setting couldn't be any better. First, he and Gretchen could dine at their favorite restaurant, Mr. Ups, the selfsame establishment where they had eaten the night they had lost their respective virginities on the couch in the music library. Then they could walk the campus, holding hands laughing over old jokes, maybe even singing show tunes from Horatio King's *Lear*. They could get silly, taking turns on the swings in front of the Student Center. Finally, arm and arm, Ben would move Gretchen to a bench by the campus Chapel (near the place he had once told her he loved her) and kiss her ever so gently. And then Ben would do it, woo her with a magical vision of their future: the five kids, George, Richard, Dorothy, Oscar, and Carolyn, each named after a different musical theater composer or lyricist; the 100-acre Cornwall farm bought with earnings from *Just Desserts*; Gretchen's continuing career as a fourth-grade teacher; Ben's as a Broadway composer and kids' book writer who commuted back and forth to the city by helicopter.

Parking the car at the village green, Ben smiled. An absurd plan? Perhaps. But why not? Gretchen was his best friend, after all, had been for years – and lives were built upon such absurdity. Why not get the entirety of his life in order right now?

With time to kill before meeting Gretchen for coffee before the book fair, Ben wandered the campus. Though he had only graduated four years earlier, it now seemed a lifetime – with a show coming to Broadway and a book in the stores, Ben felt like a man of the world, significantly older than the mere children wandering cluelessly to their classes. Still, he allowed himself to reminisce, thinking of that time when he too had been young. In his current fevered state, every building began to remind him of something he had done with Gretchen. Wright Theater where they had directed *Lear*. The Little Theater in the Student Center where Gretchen had a small role in Ben's first show, a musical fable based on Paul Bunyan. It was there that Ben showed his first potential (he thought) for inspired silliness with this lyrical exchange concerning starting up a maple sugaring business:

PAUL BUNYAN: You mean you tap?
FORD FORDSEN: Yes, with great ease!
PAUL BUNYAN: You tap the sap?
FORD FORDSEN: Yes, of the trees!

Then there was the larger student theater, home of Ben's second musical, the pretentious *Exit Strategy*, a story about a man who enters a Brigadoon-type world where nothing is allowed to change in order to keep out social ills.

By the time he met her for coffee, Ben's mind was steeped in nostalgia. Every sight held the tinged beauty of a faded postcard from a cherished vacation. That included Gretchen, of course, who, Ben decided, had never looked better. She had always been pretty – short blonde hair, blue eyes, dimples – but glowing in the aura of his current romantic mood, she looked somehow epic, no more or less than "the one." It seemed utterly reasonable, even necessary, to settle down with her. Their life together a fait accompli, it was all Ben could do to not immediately start discussing invitation fonts on the spot.

"Hey you," Gretchen said, giving him a friendly kiss on the

cheek. "Good drive up?"

No, a kiss on the cheek wouldn't do – not now. Ben leaned across the table and kissed her again, on the lips. Gretchen smiled and patted his hand. Ben smiled back.

"Yeah, I made good time. Was it hard to get off work early?"

"Nah, I took a personal day."

Of course, a personal day. For him.

Ben smiled and led the conversation to a discussion of college days, then inevitably to Horatio King and Everett Walker.

"So it sounds like rehearsals are going well."

"Yep."

"Everett Walker isn't as nutty as you thought, huh?"

"Well, he's nutty, but he's good."

"And you're in the middle of tech now?"

"Yeah. The timing worked out perfectly."

"And the first preview is when? Four days?"

"Three."

"Amazing!"

"I know, right?"

And so the conversation continued, one topic spilling over to the next, until Gretchen glanced at her watch.

"You better get to the fair. We'll meet right after."

"Good," Ben said.

Gretchen paused. "But actually... just to say it... there is something I want to talk about tonight."

Ben's heart stopped cold for a full second before pumping wildly.

"Oh? Me, too."

Gretchen seemed interested – and nervous – a good sign. Did she want to discuss the same thing?

"Really?" she said.

"Yeah, really."

"Give me a hint?"

Ben smiled, tempted to spill it then and there. But at the last second, he hesitated. After all, why not follow his plan and let his fantasy come to life – the walk across campus, the interlude on the swing set, the heartfelt talk by the chapel?

"It can wait," Ben said. "But how about you? What's on your mind?"

"Nah." Gretchen smiled mysteriously. "Let's chat tonight."

Ben nodded. He liked the way this was playing out. Obviously, he and Gretchen were of a mind. No doubt about it: this was going to be the easiest conversation ever. "Why wait until forty-three and a half," she would plead. "Can't we just get married now?"

"Mr. Ups?" Ben asked.

"You got it," Gretchen said. "Mr. Ups."

First, Ben had to get through the ostensible reason for his visit. From the way Gretchen had described it, the Middlebury Chamber of Commerce and Agrarian Society Bookfair had sounded like a good time: a handful of authors invited to beautiful Vermont during the first days of spring; book lovers traveling from throughout the state eager to buy. Easy.

The reality was somewhat different. While Ben had been under the impression that he would be one of a handful of writers, lavished with attention, he discovered upon arrival that he was one of fifty, set up at two lines of tables. Though many of the other books looked intriguing, Ben realized that he hadn't heard of any of them – a fact that led to the disheartening realization that the other authors hadn't heard of him in return. But lack of name recognition was a minor problem. The real torture came from the customers, local Vermonters who wandered up and down the aisles, deciding what to buy. They weren't bad people, far from it. In fact, there wasn't a single person who wasn't perfectly friendly. Even so, each one was an instrument of doom. A few customers, of course, picked up their copy of *The Worldwide Dessert Contest* with a cheerful, "This looks good. Can you sign it, please?" But others – most others – grabbed a copy and then read the flap while Ben sat still, trying not to look deathly uncomfortable.

"So?" a prospective buyer would ask. "What's this about? A *dessert contest?*"

"That's right," Ben would reply, whereby he would be put in the awkward position of pitching his own book, describing the contest, the roller-skating pies, the rhyme-land, and, of course, the changing desserts. Some people were intrigued and responded to Ben's sales pitch with a smiling, "Sounds good. I'll take it." But others – too many others – listened politely then embarrassedly placed the book back on the pile. Some were kind enough to say, "I'm on a budget" or "My son is too old for this, I think." Others averted their eyes and ran for the hills.

Even so, the awkwardness of schlepping to Vermont to hand-sell his book wasn't the worst of it. That was ignoring the ignominious display to his right. For sitting next to him was a writer who went by the nickname, Captain Dave. A picture book author, Dave's stories featured a talking mouse from Ripton, a small town up the mountain. Fair enough, Ben thought. No problem there. What annoyed him was his rival's outfit. Dressed as a giant mouse, complete with tail and whiskers, Captain Dave hawked his wares with aggressive enthusiasm.

"Read about Jerimiah the Mouse," he cried, jumping up and down, waving his books.

At first, Ben tried to ignore him. Did the man have no

shame? It was one thing to want to make a few sales. But to costume himself as a giant rodent to do it? That was pathetic. But to Ben's chagrin, the ploy worked. Whereas Ben got occasional customers for *The Worldwide Dessert Contest*, Captain Dave was selling books by the dozens. Ben was furious. Is that what it took to be a best-selling author these days? Would Ben have done better if he had come dressed as a giant dessert? A hot fudge sundae? A slice of banana cream pie?

When all was said and done, Ben sold twenty-one books, leaving a healthy pile on his table while Captain Dave sold out completely. There was one solace, though.

That night, he and Gretchen would laugh about it.

"He called himself what?" Gretchen would say.

"Captain Dave!"

"Did he really squeak?"

"With every sale."

They would giggle about it all the way back to Gretchen's home...

Ben glanced at his phone, registering the happy news that it was five o'clock. Time to wrap things up and get to Mr. Ups. But before he could, an attractive thirty-something woman with curly blonde hair approached the table. She had a baby in a *Bjorn* facing out and kicking, a girl.

"Hi," she called. "Am I in time?"

Ben nodded. "Sure. Want to look at a copy?"

The woman smiled. "Thank you."

The baby kicked. Ben did what his mother had trained him to do when in the presence of a mom and a newborn: compliment the baby.

"She's adorable."

"She's a handful," the woman said and laughed.

"An adorable handful then."

"I'll take that. So let's look at the book."

With that, the lady glanced at the cover. Ben sat down, ready to answer the typical questions about the plot one final time.

"What a beautiful picture," the woman said.

"Thanks."

"Lavenders and oranges. And the roller-skating pies. How cute."

Ben smiled. Maybe this would be a sale.

"Thanks. I don't do the cover art, of course. I just write the words."

"That's still plenty good."

She glanced at the cover as if to confirm something.

"So you're Ben Willis?"

Ben felt the slight buzz of an ego stroked. Had this woman heard of him?

"Uh, huh. Yeah."

"That's cool." The woman extended a hand. "I'm a friend of Gretchen's."

Ben's heart dropped. His fame had most definitely *not* preceded him.

"Oh?" Ben said. "So Gretchen told you I'd be here?"

"Yeah." The lady laughed. "We met at a Contra Dance."

Ben smiled. He didn't even know Gretchen went to such things.

"How Vermonty."

"Yeah, it is. Anyway, I'm Amy."

This time, she paused, as though she thought Ben should have heard of her.

"Ben."

They shook on it.

"So your book…"

Amy opened it and quickly skimmed the flap copy.

"Let's see. There's John Applefeller, Judge Nathaniel Barkle, Sylvester Sweet…"

"Yeah," Ben said. "Those are the main characters."

Amy grinned, embarrassedly.

"What?" Ben asked.

"Sorry, but I teach Feminist Theory at the college."

"So?"

"So…all your characters…they're men."

Ben paused. In truth, he didn't have a good answer. Amy was right: with the exceptions of Applefeller's assistant, Sweet's sister, and a few random dessert chefs, the characters were male.

"You're right, I guess," Ben said. "My next book is about a talking polar bear, I think. Maybe I'll make him a her."

"Oh, fun," Amy said. "Make her the head of something important…like the president or something."

"Right," Ben said. "Or a Society of Polar Bears' rights against global warming."

Amy laughed, politely.

"Anyway, I'm looking forward to tonight."

Ben was caught completely off guard, so much so it took him a full beat to regain his composure. Had Gretchen invited a friend?

"What?" he stammered.

"Oh, God," Amy said. "I had a feeling that Gretchen hadn't told you yet."

"Told me what exactly? That you were coming tonight?"

Ben could feel his voice shaking.

"I'm Amy."

Again, she said it like Ben should know.

"Yeah?"

"Amy Osterland."

Ben simply refused to comprehend what was now obvious.

"Yeah? Sorry, but I don't…"

Amy put her hand on his.

"Her girlfriend."

As if to mark the point, the baby drooled – directly onto Ben's book.

16

"You seem distracted."

It was the afternoon Ben returned from Middlebury, the day before the first preview. The two collaborators were in King's study, going over last-minute script changes. The main problem was with "Dark Chocolate," a song both King and Ben not so secretly hated but Everett Walker insisted upon keeping in the show.

"Distracted?"

"Yes. What happened up there in the Green Mountain State? Something with a woman, no doubt. Gretchen?"

Ben couldn't deny it.

"You might say that," he said. "A woman with a woman."

King was intrigued. "Ah, this sounds interesting. Do tell."

And so Ben spilled it all: the sighting of Mo and Nate on Instagram, the meeting with Gretchen before the book fair, the anticipation of the coming night. Then he segued to the fair itself, carefully including Captain Dave for drama's sake, and moving on to his unfortunate encounter with Amy Osterland.

"Oh, Christ!" King said. "A young mother?"

"Yep. A young mom."

"Had Gretchen ever given any indication…"

"No."

"And they met at a Contra Dance?"

"That's right."

"How Vermonty."

Ben forced a smile. "That's what I said. But that isn't even the worst of it."

"Oh, really?" King shuffled over to his chair and leaned forward expectantly. "There's more?"

Ben sighed. Now it was his turn to stand and pace.

"We had to meet at the restaurant, right? Well, Gretchen and I got there early and had a drink."

"I see where this is going," King said. "You were so pissed off you told her everything?"

Ben drew in a deep breath.

"Something like that."

King laughed. "Including George, Richard, Dorothy, Oscar, and Carolyn?"

"Yeah," Ben said. "Including them, our five kids."

He shuddered at the memory. In a way, it had been cathartic. At least he now knew that there was a part of him, however small, that wanted to be a father one day.

"I assume your ode to fatherhood didn't sway her?"

Ben shook his head.

"Nope."

"So, what did she say? Don't keep an old man waiting, I might keel over any second."

"What did she say?" Ben asked. "What you'd expect. That she'd always love me, but right now she was with Amy and she was sorry that she hadn't told me but she wanted to make sure that it was serious first. And then...well, I started to cry."

"Oh, God. Right there in front of her?"

"Yep. Right in front of her. And then Gretchen started to cry, and then Amy came in and she started to cry, too, because she's no fool and she figured out what was going on and got caught up in the emotion."

"What happened then?"

Ben laughed. "Aside from everyone looking at us like someone had died?"

"Yes, aside from that."

"I finally began to pull it together, I guess. Then I made a joke about little Oscar – you know, one of our non-existent future kids – and we all started to laugh. Suddenly, the whole thing seemed absurd, and the spell broke. I realized that I only thought I was in love with her. I mean, I am in love with her. I always will be, but I'm maybe not quite ready and she is."

"Yes," King said with a sage nod. "And she likes women, it seems."

Ben sighed. "Yeah, that, too."

Indeed, the spell had broken. Ben hadn't been in love with Gretchen, not really – he knew that now. He just wanted her to be available when he was ready. Toward the end of the week, she had sent a text: "Still friends?" Ben had answered, "Yes, indeed" and even meant it. Even so, Ben missed the possibility of some sort of perfect future waiting for him at age forty-three and a half. Now he was on his own.

King sighed. "Well, as I said, you're better off without her – as a romantic interest, anyway."

"I suppose I have no choice."

"I suppose not," King said. "You have Mo anyway. And she'll be back from London soon enough."

"She has a boyfriend," Ben said. "I told you about that."

King was unconvinced. "She doesn't like him as much as you."

"Oh, really?" Ben said. "You know this how?"

King laughed. "Willis, you're a fool. I saw the look in her eyes that night at Sir Sanabelle's mansion. That's how! That girl was seriously smitten."

Ben shrugged. True or not, it didn't seem to matter now – not with Mo on another continent with another guy.

"Anyway," King said, after waiting an appropriate amount of time to change the subject. "Enough of your rather strange love life. What do we do with Dark Chocolate?"

Ben knew what he wanted to do. Again, King saw right through him.

"Don't tell me."

Ben shrugged.

"The workshop?" King said.

"They can only hate it. Maybe someone will say something smart?"

King sighed. During the rewrites and endless meetings, Ben had been impressed by the old man's stamina. But though King had gone strong through many long days and nights of work, for one of the first times since they had met, he looked his age.

"What do you think?" Ben asked.

Ben expected King to reject the idea out of hand as he had before, most likely with a string of expletives. Instead, the old man sighed.

"Well," he said. "Ethan Hancock is a pretentious fool but he's certainly no idiot."

"True," Ben said. "I suppose it couldn't hurt. Our backs are against the wall with this song." Then he paused and suggested the wholly improbable. "Maybe you'd like to come with me? Ethan left an open invitation. The class would go nuts to meet you."

King smiled wanly. "They might make us write an 'I Want' song about a missionary who wants to have relations with a water buffalo."

178

Ben laughed. "That actually could be pretty good." He paused. "Of course, I understand if you don't want to see Ethan."

King grunted. "That bastard puts down my music. Isn't that what you told me?"

"Well, only once really. Mostly, he's respectful." Ben paused. "Anyway, how often have you seen him since…?"

His voice trailed off.

"Since when?" King said. "Since our misguided affair blew up?"

Ben nodded.

"I've seen the fool around town now and then," King said. "He's pretentious but mostly harmless – when he's not trashing my work or copying my music."

Then King said something surprising. "But as much as I hate to admit it." He paused, scratched Juniper then pushed him to the floor. "As much as I hate to admit it, my impromptu therapy session on the plane made me realize the extent to which I blame Ethan for Richard's and my breakup. And that, I realize now, is unfair. The fault there was mine."

It was a huge admission; one Ben knew that King didn't make lightly.

"So come to the class," Ben said. "Patch things up. My classmates will freak."

King scratched his beard. "It might be fun to meet the students." He shook his head. "But no, you go and report back what the rabble says. I'll stay here with Juniper."

"You're sure?" Ben said.

King nodded. "You know how I get. I might shoot off my mouth. Make a spectacle. Ethan has his charm but he's insufferable." King laughed. "And so am I, I guess. Not a good combination."

And so Ben walked across town to the AMI building on 57th Street by himself then scrawled his name and the title "Dark Chocolate" on the workshop song list and waited to be called. But at number eight in the queue, he had to sit through his classmates playing songs from their musicals. Billy Hansen went first, singing the opening number from *Oldies But Goodies*, a show set in a futuristic old-age home. A while later Tiffany Holt played a ballad from her musical *17!* based on the movie *Stalag 17*. Jen Rosenthal performed a comedy number from her show about a blind clown who falls in love with a tightrope walker. Throughout, the class's comments ranged from cutting to clueless to genuinely insightful, with Ethan leading the charge. At five forty with Steve Andrews ahead of him, Ben assumed he would have to wait a week to present. But when Steve decided his lyric wasn't ready ("My inner rhymes feel pedestrian"), Ben had his chance.

"All right then," Ethan said, looking down at his list. "One more today. Mr. Willis?"

As always when he was called on to present, Ben's heart began to race, nerves being part of the workshop. Tiffany Holt had once thrown up on the way to the keyboard. But this time, Ben was even more anxious than usual. Generally, when he presented a song, he had some hopes that it would be good. This time he knew what he was about to play was terrible. (How could it be otherwise with an opening line that still rhymed "shit" with "chocolate"?) He just needed the class to tell him why and suggest a way to make it better so he and King could fix it during previews. Still, who wanted to lay himself out for a public flaying with poor material? No one. There was still time to get out of it, shift gears, say he wasn't ready and opt-out, but Ben found himself rising shakily to his feet, murmuring "that's right," then cutting through the classroom to the piano.

The class looked at him expectantly.

"So," Ben began, shakily. "This is from *Just Desserts*. I'm having trouble with a lyric."

Ben saw glances exchanged around the room. Were they salivating, waiting for a chance to rip him to shreds? Probably.

"A song in Act Two is still giving us problems," Ben went on.

"You came to the right place," Ethan said.

"Did you write the music?" Tiffany Holt asked even though she already knew the answer. "Or was it…" Her voice trailed off, almost too awestruck to utter his name.

"Yes," Ben said. "Horatio King."

An audible gasp filled the room. Though everyone knew that Ben was collaborating with the great man, something about it was too incongruous to truly believe, as if they needed the fact confirmed every single time the subject arose.

"So you'll be playing his music on piano?" Steve Andrews asked.

"Trying," Ben said.

"Good," Ethan said, matter-of-factly. "Now what's the song about? Give us the set-up."

"Let's see," Ben began, shakily. "As you know, the show is about this guy named John Applefeller. This is a song he sings in the second act when he feels the urge to win getting too strong."

It was a simple introduction but all that Ben thought was needed. He straightened himself in his seat, played a random chord, then began. Horatio King's music was known to be difficult with an especially tricky left hand. Thankfully, this piece was on the easy side. Good by ear at the piano, Ben had been able to memorize the accompaniment. Singing was another issue altogether. Ben could carry a tune, there was that much, but his tone left something to be desired.

He stopped playing and looked up, scanning the expectant faces of the crowded room. Ben didn't know if he had ever heard a silence more charged – a silence so quiet it was almost loud, ringing in his ears.

"Anytime," Ethan said.

The class chuckled, uneasily.

Ben felt a trickle of sweat drip down his arm. He looked back out to the class then played the introduction once again, loud and clear.

Then he heard a voice.

"Where is it then? That door? Good!"

Ben inhaled sharply. The members of the class exchanged glances that bordered on disbelief.

"Holy shit," Billy Hansen whispered. "Is that who I think it is?"

"Do I really look that old?" King was saying now to some unfortunate who had obviously offered to help. "I can still walk. Out of my way, thank you very much!"

A split second later, the door burst open. In he stepped, a cane in one hand and a leash in the other. Juniper wagged his tail.

"Mr. King," Ben stammered. "Juniper." The dog yapped a seeming greeting. "You came."

"Surprised?" King said.

"A little," Ben said.

In truth, he was worried. Was there a wobble in the old man's step? Had he been drinking? He didn't think so. But with Horatio King, all bets were off.

"I was walking Juniper when I got an idea of something else we could perform," the old man replied. "Something better than that Dark Chocolate monstrosity. Jumped right in a cab."

Before Ben – or anyone else for that matter – could respond, Juniper barked again, pulling his master toward the front of the room.

"Well, well," Ethan said with a forced smile. "Good to see you, Horatio. Welcome."

King bowed slightly. "Ethan."

Ben sighed, somewhat relieved. At least the two men were being polite.

"Meet Horatio King everyone," Ethan went on.

Though Johnny Framingham managed an anemic "hi" everyone else was dumbstruck, too amazed to say a word.

"Sorry about butting in," King said. "But Ben said I should drop by. And it looks like I came just in time."

All eyes were on King as though a deity had just entered their presence. Then Ethan asked what everyone was wondering.

"You're going to play for us?"

King bowed slightly. "I'd be honored."

The class sighed as one and applauded. Excited, Juniper jumped to Ben's lap, licked him furiously, and then scampered around the room, forcing Steve Andrews to give chase, eventually scooping the dog into his arms by Jen Rosenthal's feet.

"Got you, you little shit," King said as Steve handed him back his poodle. "Yes, I'll play," he went on but then smiled mischievously, a change of expression that caused Ben to be instantly apprehensive. He knew all too well of King's inability to keep his thoughts to himself or to let go of a satisfying grudge. The old man's gaze found Ethan. "I'll play if you're sure that you want the composer whose music is 'harmonically stagnant' to perform for your class."

A low gasp filled the room. Stunned, Ethan Hancock glared at Ben and then blushed. Ben shuddered. Had King decided to come to the class to have it out with Ethan once and for all? Was that the real reason he had hustled over?

To his credit, Ethan contained himself with a forced smile. "I sometimes exaggerate to make a point." He paused, and took a breath. "You know I have the utmost respect for your work."

"Thank you, kindly. If that's an apology, I accept it."

"It is."

"Good."

Ben felt a second of relief – but only a second because now it was Ethan's turn to grin. It was as if something had occurred to him, he wasn't quite sure he should say, a golden opportunity not to be missed.

"Of course," Ethan said. "We've all had our bad days."

King narrowed his eyes. "What's that supposed to mean?"

"Just that. Everyone knows about your great works but wouldn't it be educational if you were to tell the class a little bit about some of your lesser efforts?" Now he grinned more broadly. "*In Dubious Battle,* for instance?"

King blinked. "*In Dubious Battle?*"

"*Hmm hmm.*"

"Why that hardly counts as serious work," King sputtered. "It died in workshop. No one was supposed to hear it."

"Everybody's heard it," Ethan said.

"I have the bootleg," Johnny Framingham said.

"Me too," Billy Hansen said.

"Kindly burn them," King said.

"But I like parts of it," Johnny said.

King shuddered and turned back to Ethan.

"So you don't like *In Dubious Battle.* That's all you've got?

184

Even I admit it was God awful."

"Not God awful, Mr. King," Johnny said. "Interesting."

"My boy," King said. "Interesting is usually a euphemism for God awful." He turned back to Ethan. "What else do you take issue with? Surely not *Lear* or *Twice Upon a Time*?"

"No, no," Ethan said. "Those are masterpieces."

"Then what?" King asked.

Ethan shrugged. "Well, I don't like to say it…"

"No, come on!" King said, tapping his cane on the hard floor. "You brought it up. Let's have this out."

"In front of the class?" Ethan said.

"Fuck yes! They love it, right?"

King looked at the students. No one nodded, but no one disagreed either.

"If you insist," Ethan said. "Some of your early work tries too hard to be innovative. And then, well…*Black Hawk Down*, Horatio?"

To Ben's horror, someone in the class laughed in agreement. King peered over the room like a peeved kindergarten teacher. Then he turned back to Ethan.

"Maybe *Black Hawk* flopped," King snapped his words off like dry kindling. "But at least when I miss the music is my own!"

Ethan's eyes went wide. Ben shuddered, wishing he could disappear into the piano keys. This was worse than he ever could have imagined. Low gasps filled the room.

"My own?" Ethan said. "What are you suggesting?

"*Stepping Out*?"

"What of it?"

"How much of it is actually yours?"

The class went stone quiet. Was Horatio King mocking the musical that had won a Tony for best score?

"All of it," Ethan said, coldly. "Every last note."

"Every last note?" King said. "The opening number? What's it called again?"

"'Welcome to Detroit.'"

"Right. 'Welcome to Detroit.'" King faced the class. "Pure Andrew Lloyd Webber!"

Ethan lurched to his feet.

"Webber? Not on your life. It's mine through and through."

"If that's what you want to think," King said, waving his cane. "But Webber's gaudy influence couldn't be more apparent."

"Influence maybe," Ethan said. "A little. But hardly stolen."

"We're all influenced by the generations before," Johnny Framingham said bravely.

"Exactly," Ethan said. "Influenced is how one generation of artists informs the next. It's how an art form grows and survives. Everyone is influenced by everyone. Even you, Horatio."

King lurched around to face his accuser. "Me?"

"Yes," Ethan said.

"Name the measure!"

Ethan smiled. "As gorgeous as it is, don't tell me you don't hear traces of Gershwin in *Twice Upon a Time*?"

The class shuddered.

"The hell you do!"

Ben thought King was going to brain Ethan with his cane.

"The way you toggle from major to minor in the overture," Ethan said.

"Oh, fuck it," King said, scratching his beard. "Everyone plays with major and minor, that's nothing."

"My point exactly," Ethan said. "We're all influenced by the greats. Just like many people in this classroom are influenced by you."

"Influence is one thing," King fumed. "Down and out copying is another. Some of your *Stepping Out* is lifted from Verdi! And some... some is from me!"

"From you?"

The class was riveted. This was high drama of the first order, better than a premium seat to Broadway's hottest show.

"Yes! From *Proust*!"

"*Proust*?" Ethan said. "We wrote six songs, all of them bad."

"Don't deny it," King insisted. "My opening number in D-flat."

"Everyone writes in D-flat," Ethan said. "It's my favorite key."

King waved a hand. "Mine too! You took the main melody that I wrote, inverted it, and put it in your opening to Act Two. Don't think I didn't hear it because I have ears of fucking gold."

"Yes, that melody was inverted," Ethan exclaimed. "But you're forgetting: it was my melody to begin with."

"Not true," the old man said. "Not true."

To that, he pushed Ben to the side of the piano bench and then played the eight-note melody the way it had been originally written. He looked at the class.

"Tell me if that's not pure Horatio King!"

Without waiting for an answer, he inverted the melody, syncopating it.

"And that," King went on, "is the opening of Act Two of *Stepping Out*!"

"Which I still say I wrote," Ethan said. "Both melodies!"

"Not how I remember it," King said. "Worse, you took my perfectly nice tune and perverted it into something crass and commercial."

"Commercial, my ass," Ethan said. "Yes, the inverted melody may be a little bit more mainstream, but it still has integrity. You know what your problem is, Horatio. It isn't that I steal because I don't and you know that deep down. Or that I'm influenced by others because everyone is a little. It's that I don't give up. I've had my flops too, everyone has, but at least I'm out there taking my cuts. Still writing!"

"I'm writing now," King said.

"Yes," Ethan cried. "After fifteen years of getting soused!"

Suddenly, everyone was talking at once, amazed and more than a little bit embarrassed by what they had just witnessed. As for Ben, he sat at the piano slumped over like he had been shot. Then, just like that, Juniper leaped onto a desk then at Ethan's head. A second later, the angry poodle was on the teacher's shoulder, chewing his sleeve.

"Someone get this damned beast off me!"

Johnny and Billy shot to their feet, but King waved them back with his cane.

"Relax," he shouted. "It's just a mutt giving your teacher no more than what he deserves! Juniper! Come now!"

With another loud snarl, Juniper sprung to King.

"Your dog attacked me," Ethan whined, stating the obvious. "I should have you incarcerated!"

"For what?" King replied, laying Juniper back on the piano. "Speaking the truth?"

Ethan blinked. "You liked my music well enough back in the day."

"Yes, some of your music was first rate," King said. "Truly excellent! But then you wrote *Stepping Out* and sold out. And for your information, with the exception of two plane trips and one cast party, I haven't had a drink these past three months. Isn't that right, Ben?"

Ben couldn't be precisely sure – part of him suspected he was at least a little bit drunk right then – but nodded anyway. "Right."

"See!"

"All right, all right," Ethan said. "I apologize for the accusation. And I apologize for putting down your music to the class. I can be that way sometimes. Call it professional jealousy mixed with a naturally sarcastic nature. I don't care for *Black Hawk Down,* but the music isn't harmonically stagnant – at least not most of it. Fair enough?"

To Ben's surprise, Ethan extended his hand. King hesitated. There was a split second where Ben thought he might spit on his palm rather than shake it. Instead, King took a deep breath.

"And I suppose I apologize for saying you stole my music. Maybe I'm misremembering. And much of your music is quite original. I wish you'd get back to it."

"Well…fair enough."

The two men finally shook. And as they did, the students applauded. As the cheering grew, the two men faced the class awkwardly. Ben had never felt more relieved.

"And with that, it appears that today's melodrama is over," Ethan said with a smile.

"Curtain."

"Yes," King said with a slight bow. "Curtain."

"But one more thing," Ethan said. "I have a question for you." The teacher gestured impatiently toward the piano. "Did you come here to play or argue?"

"Maybe a little bit of both," King said with a laugh. Then he narrowed his eyes. "You just want the chance to rip me to shreds."

"Only if you deserve it."

King looked to Ben.

"You played them the intro already?"

Ben nodded. "Yes, but I was about to stop."

"Good," King said. "We hardly need the class to tell us that 'Dark Chocolate' stinks. The lyric is awful, and the music is shit. That's why I hustled over here. I don't want you to play it. In fact, I've spoken to Everett Walker. It's cut from the show."

"It is?" Ben said. "Just like that?"

"I threatened to withdraw my entire score if he didn't," King said. "Now let's play something else. The new song for the end."

"What? 'Simple Desserts?'"

"Yes, why not that one?"

Ben shrugged. "Fine with me. But I've only written the lyrics. I don't know the music."

King laughed. "Don't worry, son." He pointed to his head. "I know it. That's why I bustled over here. I heard the tune in my head while walking Juniper. Wanted to share it with you right away. Thought it was a good opportunity to meet your friends. Now out of my way."

As the class clapped yet again, King sat at the piano. Juniper settled to the old man's side.

"All right then," King said. "This is from the end of our show. All you really need to know is that after a whole bunch of pyrotechnics, including roller-skating and flying pies, Applefeller, our hero, has won the contest with a simple apple pie."

And King began to play. It was beautiful, and simple with notable King touches of dissonance to keep it interesting. Then the old man raised his gravelly baritone and began to sing:

After the pies have flown
Cartwheeled across the sky.
The dessert that won it all.
Is a pie that was just a pie.

Through all the changing years
Of failure and dismay
The Silver Spoon was there
A simple dessert away.

Simple desserts, my friend.
Simple desserts, my friend.
That's what's in your plan.
A simple dessert came through
For a simply lovely man.

King sang all three verses. When he was done, the class was silent. Was it the best Horatio King melody ever? No. But it was beautiful nonetheless, rising and falling naturally, simple in its directness yet surprising when it had to be.

"So?" King asked when he was done, looking at Ethan. "Harmonically stagnant?"

Ethan shook his head. "No, Horatio. It's lovely."

The class agreed.

"I loved it," Johnny said.

"The progression from E major to F sharp was particularly effective," Steve Andrews commented.

"Ha!" King said, clearly pleased.

Then, to Ben's surprise, Ethan Hancock cleared his throat and turned to the class. "Despite things I might have said throughout the year, Horatio King is one of the great talents in the history of musical theater."

The class applauded again. King nodded happily, clearly pleased. He looked at Ben and winked. Then he turned to the class.

"And let me say that I've been too harsh to Ben about this workshop. I see now what fine work you do."

"The class goes for drinks sometimes after class," Ethan said. "Now that today's session is through, perhaps you'd like to join?"

To his surprise, Ben saw Ethan and King's gaze linger for a long moment. Was he sensing a renewed friendship?

"I would be delighted. But if it's okay with you, no hard stuff for me. Just soda."

Ethan smiled. "Of course. Come on, class. Before Horatio changes his mind. Let's get out of here."

Horatio King beckoned to Juniper and took one step toward the door. Then he wrinkled his brow inquisitively as though he had just thought of something funny to say, then sighed once, and collapsed to the floor.

17

If Johnny Framingham and Jen Rosenthal hadn't known CPR, the great man might not have made it. Thankfully, the two students were able to keep King going until the EMTs rushed him to New York Hospital. Now Ben was rushing himself, from the Imperial Theater to King's room in the intensive care unit. The curtain had just gone down on the first preview of *Just Desserts*. Unable to flag a cab or get an Uber and ceding to King's demand to hear the news in person, Ben was scurrying like a madman through traffic, thinking about the show. The first performance had started so well – the excitement of seeing his name on the marquee, the thrill of reading his bio in the Playbill, and the buzz of anticipation as the audience took their seats. If only Ben could have felt more sanguine about what he had actually seen on stage! At the very least, he had expected *Just Desserts* to be a good time, an upbeat extravaganza with thrilling dances and good tunes. The elements were all there, the music well arranged, the lyrics whimsical, the choreography vigorous, the pies roller-skating like mad. But by the end of the opening number, Ben saw just how a shift in tone could leech the life out of a piece of theater. Yes, the staged iteration of *Just Desserts* had added depth – Everett Walker had delivered that in spades – but it was also dimly lit, over-acted, and heavy-handed, all at the expense of a light touch. At least that's what Ben had thought. Still, like a dying man hoping for a last-minute reprieve, the young man continued his mad sprint across town, praying that he had misread the performance. The audience had applauded after most of the songs, hadn't it? No one had walked out. The ovation at the end had been enthusiastic enough. On the other hand, weren't Broadway audiences these days trained to applaud wildly whether they had enjoyed a show or not?

With the hospital in the distance, Ben paused to catch his breath, then jogged easily across the street. A moment later, he was walking briskly up the circular driveway to the hospital's entrance, then past the information desk and gift shop into the elevator. On the 7th floor, intensive care unit, he heard the old man before he saw him.

"Where the devil is the punk?"

Apparently, the nurse on duty was confused.

"The doctor, you mean?" he said. "She's making rounds. Should be here soon."

"Oh, not her! Oh, hell."

The sound of a baseball game – the Mets – wafted down the hall. Probably too exhausted to read, King was passing the time any way he could.

"Sorry," another nurse said to Ben. "Visiting hours are pretty much over."

"But I have to see Mr. King."

"Ben?" King called. Clearly, his hearing aid was in complete working order even if his heart wasn't. "Is that you?"

"Yes."

"Let him in," the old man called. "Let him in!"

Ben pushed by the nurse and all but fell into the room. King was lying back in a hospital bed. An IV in his arm, he was hooked up to a steadily beeping heart monitor.

"You okay?" King asked.

"Couldn't get a cab," Ben said. "I ran."

"All the way?"

Ben nodded.

"If you feel woozy, you came to the right place. They have respirators. Sit. I've been waiting, watching baseball. I hate baseball. Now talk. How'd it go?"

Ben collapsed onto the straight-backed chair by King's bed. "How'd it go?"

"Speak, man." A tube up his nose, King barked the words as loudly as he could. "Do we have a hit?"

Ben didn't know how to begin. What does one say to an ailing icon hooked up to a heart monitor? The truth? That after walking into the theater with the strut of a conquering hero, that he had expected more?

"Well," he began. "The crowd applauded a lot."

King pressed a button on the side of his bed. A soft whirr brought him upright. He looked tired, sick, but his eyes were alive, twinkling even. Ben saw then and there how badly he wanted this hit – maybe even more than he did.

"They did?" King said. "That's good. Applause is good."

"But then…"

"Then what?"

"They sort of didn't."

King frowned. "They didn't? Where?"

Ben could no longer completely mask his disappointment. "It's hard to say exactly. Here and there."

King blinked. "I don't understand. They liked the overture, didn't they?"

"Oh, yes," Ben said. "There was applause after that."

"And 'The Man with the Changing Desserts?' That's a damned fine opening number."

"It is," Ben said. "But…"

"But what?"

"It was sort of dimly lit."

"Could you see anything?"

"Mostly shadows."

King shook his head. "Damnit! I told Everett we needed a sunnier palate. Did the audience laugh at least?"

Ben wanted to answer that the audience had howled – both because he wished that had been what had happened but also because he worried the naked truth might give the great Horatio King another coronary.

"It's a simple question, boy. During the opening number. Did they laugh?"

"Some," Ben managed. "They liked Judge Barkle's entrance. They laughed at him."

"At the actor or the apple on his face?"

"Hard to tell. I think the apple. And Sylvester Sweet got a good response."

"Of course he did."

"They liked it when he cooked the double-chocolate-raspberry-coconut-lime swirl on stage."

"How about Act Two when he sang 'The King of Dessert?'"

Ben nodded. "Good round of applause."

King seemed encouraged. "This doesn't sound so terrible. And when the pie's roller-skated?"

"Yes, applause," Ben said truthfully. "Lots of it. Even a few gasps. More when they flew."

King scratched his beard, visibly relieved now. "Sounds as though it went pretty well for a first preview."

"Yeah," Ben said. "I guess it went fine."

King raised an eyebrow. "You guess it went fine? Come on, kid. The truth. I can take it. I promise not to croak in front of you."

Ben stood up. "Okay, yeah, there were some laughs and there were some high points…"

His voice trailed off.

"But?" King asked.

Ben sighed. "But all in all, the whole thing was so gloomy."

"Gloomy?" King said. "Well, it is supposed to have a darkness to it."

"Darkness, sure, a little bit," Ben said. "But not two AM at the jazz club."

King frowned. "The lighting was that bad?"

Ben was pacing now. "It was as though Everett Walker listened to Sven Nordgren more than us. Then again, the last show I wrote was performed for eighty people at the Little Theater at Middlebury College. What do I know?"

King looked concerned. For a split second, Ben wished Juniper had been there for the old man to either pet or push off the bed – anything to comfort him.

"You might know more than you think," King said, stroking his beard. "If you felt the audience hesitating perhaps it's true. Get my laptop. It's under my bed."

"Your laptop?" Ben asked. "Why?"

King sighed. "I think we have no choice."

"No choice for what?"

The old man seemed almost too embarrassed to suggest it. He looked back to the TV for a split second where a Met was taking a called third strike, then turned back to Ben.

"Chatrooms."

Ben blinked. "Chatrooms? People will have posted…already?"

"Yes, already. Of course, already! The vultures come out

right away. So do the fans. Come on, let's see if your instincts are right. Get the computer."

Ben did as he was told. In the moment it took him to log on and find the hospital's internet provider and passcode, the next Met up to the plate got a game-winning single, a victory Ben took as a good omen.

"Nice win," Ben said.

"Fuck the Mets," King said. "Go to *BroadwaySpeaks* first. That's where people post right after an opening, right?"

"That and a few others," Ben said.

"Well, open it."

Again, Ben did as he was told. With the computer in his lap, he typed in *BroadwaySpeaks* and clicked on *New York Chatroom*.

"Well?" King asked. "Do we have a thread yet?"

Ben scanned the page. Not only did they have a thread but it was the first in the queue, clearly recently added.

"We do."

"What's it say?"

Ben read, "*Did Anyone See the First Preview of Just Desserts?*"

"Has anyone responded?" King asked.

"There are a few comments, actually. The first is from *SeesEverything*."

"Well, come on, man. Out with it."

Ben's heart was beating so fast he forced himself to pause and draw in a deep breath.

"What's wrong? I'm a dying man here."

"Sorry, just nervous," Ben said.

"Come on, kid. Man up."

Fingers trembling, Ben clicked on the thread. He had been

expecting a few lines on the show, more of a passing comment than a full-fledged review. Instead, he was confronted with a solid block paragraph.

"Is there anything there?"

"Yes," Ben said. "And by someone who can type very quickly."

"Read it!"

Ben cleared his throat.

"What to say about Horatio King's new show, a quasi-kids'-mash up that isn't sure what it wants to be or why it even exists."

"Fucker," King said.

Ben shuddered. "Oh, my God, that's brutal."

"That's how these guys can be," King said. "Assholes. But it's like ripping off a Band-Aid. Better to read it quickly and get it over with. The sooner we know what the public really thinks about the show, the sooner we can fix it."

"So I should go on then?"

"Yes, yes. Go on!"

Ben drew in a deep breath, forcing himself to be calm, reminding himself it was only one opinion.

"The problem isn't in the music," Ben read, "which is perfectly pleasant if you like late-era Rodgers and Hammerstein. The lyrics aren't terrible either (written by newcomer Ben Willis). They have occasional wit and whimsy to spare. The book? Well, it's fine, too, I guess – some funny lines where officious judges judge different oddly named desserts like a double-chocolate-crème-strawberry-rhubarb tart."

"Oh, Christ," King said. "It's a double-chocolate-fudge-raspberry-coconut-lime swirl!"

"I know," Ben said.

"These bloggers," King said. "They don't know anything.

Late Rodgers and Hammerstein? What the hell is that?"

"Stupid," Ben said (though he had taken it as something of a complement. Was being compared to *Flower Drum Song* and *The Sound of Music* so bad?). "Should I keep reading?"

"Yes, I can handle it. Go ahead."

"No, the trouble with the misguided *Just Desserts*," Ben read, "isn't in its component parts. The music, lyrics and book are passably fine. If it hadn't been a Horatio King production, I might even say they were good. No, the problem is that the show is good but just not good enough."

"Oh, hell," King said.

"Should I stop? There's more."

Ben scanned down the page – there was a lot more, an entire single-spaced page worth. With a glance, Ben picked up random phrases such as "passably atrocious," "wretchedly maudlin," and "nice try."

"*SeesEverything* is a jackass," King said. "The next thread."

"You're sure?" Ben asked with a glance toward the heart monitor. Was it was beeping more rapidly?

King nodded. "Stop worrying, I can take it."

Ben clicked to the next link.

"This is by *HatesEverything*."

"God help me," King muttered.

"Absurd lightweight return to the Great White Way for Horatio King," Ben read.

"Fuck it," King said. "What do you expect from someone who names himself *HatesEverything*? Go down the list."

"I thought you wanted to hear everything?"

"Yes, but no need to stick a pin in the eye if not necessary. Down the list. One of them has to be good."

Dutifully, Ben clicked.

"What's this one called?" King asked.

"*DreamCurly.*"

"*DreamCurly?*" King nodded, apparently encouraged. "No one who names him or herself after a Rodgers and Hammerstein character can be that vicious. Go ahead, read."

Ben began, "*Just Desserts* had its first preview at the Imperial last night and I was there. Poorly directed and poorly lit, I might have enjoyed this new Horatio King presentation if I had been able to see the stage. Everett Walker, known predominantly for his avant-garde productions of Shakespeare, has taken a shot at a bright, new musical comedy – even doing the choreography himself – and failed. Dark, dreary, depressing – these and other similar adjectives come to mind to describe the production – a show that manages to make roller-skating-apple-pies, a charming device, ludicrous with gaudy lighting effects and even, dare I say it, smoke machines."

"Stop!" King shouted.

Ben closed the computer. King glared at him, eyes wide.

"The show? It was that bad?"

"Aren't bloggers always negative?"

"Yes, and bitchy to the extreme. But that doesn't mean they're all morons. Dark, dreary and depressing, was it?"

Ben opened the computer back up and looked back to the text. "Um, yeah."

King shook himself.

"We're doomed."

"Wait," Ben said, scanning down the list. "Here's a good one."

"Truly? You aren't just playing with an old man's fragile mind?"

"No, it's good, Listen."

Ben read:

"*Just Desserts* at the Imperial is a delight. How nice to welcome Horatio King back to Broadway. This is an extravaganza that features a dessert genius who talks in rhymes and roller-skating pies. Flying ones, too! How they pulled it off, I can't imagine. Wires, I suppose. There's a story here, too, a good one of faith and redemption, based on a kids' novel by Ben Willis. All in all, a thrilling display of wit, story-telling, and stage magic. Highly recommended."

Ben looked to King expectantly.

"Who wrote that? Your mommy?"

In truth, Ben's mom had been at the performance. As far as he knew, she didn't visit chat rooms.

"I don't think so."

"Then who? *LikesEverything*?"

Ben laughed. "No," he said. "It's by *ShowTuneNerd*."

"*ShowTuneNerd*, huh?" King said, gruffly. "At least there's one fan."

"Oh, wait," Ben said. "Maybe there's one more. Another post just showed up."

"Who from."

"*MalvolioLover*."

"*MalvolioLover*?" King said. "This is as far from Shakespeare as the Earth is from the third moon of Jupiter. Get ready for another slam job."

"Maybe not. Should I read it?"

King sighed. "Go ahead. Drive a fork through my damaged ventricles."

Ben clicked on the link. Depressed by the response to the show, he didn't know if he had the fortitude to take even one more negative review. For Ben knew full well what would happen if this show was a flop: he would be remembered (if at all) as a footnote in musical theater history, the kid who somehow convinced an aging icon to cap off his career with a children's show. The butt of a joke.

"So read."

Ben cleared his throat. What choice did he have?

"Last night a show brimming with stunning potential opened for its first preview at the Imperial Theater. That show is *Just Desserts*, music by Horatio King, lyrics and book by newcomer, Ben Willis. To say I was excited is an understatement. Quivering would be more like it. Now onto the show: I'm happy to say that there is potential here. Good songs, clever lyrics, a sympathetic leading man (John Applefeller who desperately wants to win a dessert contest, of all things, but it works, played by a charming Joe Brady). The trouble is that the production values and some of the writing don't match the show's overall tone. The villain is a mock-up of a dictator. The judges are crazed and rapacious men on the take. This and other heavy-handed devices pervade. That would be okay if the piece called for them. Alas, it doesn't. Director/Choreographer Everett Walker has weighed the material down with schemes more suited to some of his brilliant Shakespearean interpretations. But this is light, American musical theater. One hopes that the producers, writers, and directors gather forces to fix what could be a fine little musical by opening night, one that could bring joy to children and their parents alike."

Ben looked to King. "That seems fair."

But King wasn't listening. Instead, he was shaking – Ben couldn't tell if it was with anger or delight.

"What? Are you okay? Should I call the nurse?"

"That post," King said.

"Yes, it was helpful, don't you think?"

"I think I know the author," King choked.

"Oh, really?"

"It was his favorite role."

"What was?"

"Malvolio."

"Who?" Ben asked.

King looked stunned, as if he was just wrapping his mind around something too hard to believe.

"Who?" Ben repeated.

King's eyes went wide. "It's Richard!"

18

Ben slept poorly that night, worrying about the show, yes, but also wondering about Richard Sinclair. As far-fetched as it seemed, had Horatio been correct? Was Richard really *MalvolioLover*? If so, it raised many questions.

1. Had King's old lover attended the preview hoping to run into him? Probably yes.

2. Was it word of King's heart attack – common knowledge in the Broadway community – that had spurred Richard to take action? Probably yes, again.

3. And most importantly: Would Richard have written a leading post on *BroadwaySpeaks* if he didn't still have unresolved feelings toward King? Certainly not.

At least that's what Ben thought. Which is why that morning, after his coffee and croissant, Ben did what he knew King would be too proud to do himself. Clicking back on *BroadwaySpeaks* he wrote a follow up to *MalvolioLover's* post:

"I'll be at the theater this afternoon. Come find me for more news of the King.

Best, Willis"

Now mid-afternoon, Ben hustled to the theater for the second preview, wondering if Richard had received his message. If he had, would he realize what Ben had meant? Would he show up? Keeping his eyes peeled, Ben maneuvered his way down 45th Street, throwing himself into the brunt of the Saturday matinee rush. Skirting past a line for *Dalmatians* (it wended around the corner from the Avery Theater into Schubert Alley), Ben hit a bottleneck in front of a revival of O'Neill's *The Iceman Cometh,* cut into the street itself, slid around a line of cabs, and walked the final twenty feet to the Imperial. There Ben got his first truly good news of the day. From the looks of the crowd, word of the previous night's debacle hadn't spread – at least not yet. In fact, to Ben's surprise, the line for entry into *Just Desserts* stretched from the box office most of the way to 8th Avenue. Apparently, ticket holders were still eager to see the new Horatio King show, regardless of what the chatrooms had reported the night before. Instead of irate patrons angrily demanding their money back at the box office (something Ben had imagined), there was a buzz in the air, that indefinable excitement that ignited a crowd convinced they were about to see a hit.

"Yes," Ben said quietly to himself.

He looked to the marquee with newfound hope:

JUST DESSERTS
Music by Horatio King
Book and Lyrics by Ben Willis

Maybe it could be a success, after all? In a world where *Dalmatians* was still packing them in, why not?

With a few minutes to go before he had to enter the theater, Ben planted himself by the stage door and kept an eye out for Richard Sinclair. As with all Broadway shows, a healthy smattering of elderly people, so-called "blue hairs," were on line, milling about. But every man who fit Richard's general age range was either too short, too wide, or too poorly dressed. Certainly, none had Sinclair's elegance or TV star good looks. (One man was wearing a Knicks' sweatshirt). While keeping half an eye out for Richard, Ben drank in the atmosphere, allowing himself to believe that the night before hadn't really happened at all, that he and King weren't sitting on a potential embarrassment but a hit of epic proportions.

"Ben! There you are, dear boy!"

Bustling his way through the crowd was Maria Feltenstein, the British producer Ben had met at the home of Eric Sanabelle. Dressed down for the matinee, she wore a simple skirt, a yellow blouse, and a blue scarf.

"Jolly good show last night," she said, breathlessly. "Jolly good."

Ben blinked. Had he heard correctly? "Really? You think?"

"Were there problems?" she replied. "Of course, there were. The pace, of course. Need to speed it up. And some of the jokes aren't landing. But don't worry. We have two weeks of previews. Plenty of time to do the work and get everything in shape. I predict great reviews."

Ben liked what he was hearing.

"Did Walker spend the morning adjusting the lights?"

Maria nodded. "Oh, yes. He called a rehearsal."

Ben blinked. "Wait. He did? Why didn't..."

"All very last minute," Maria said quickly. "Everyone knows you've been taking such good care of Horatio."

True, but that still didn't excuse being shut out. He was one of the authors, after all.

"Walker was in rare form," Maria went on. "Along with the technical worries, he tweaked performances and dances throughout. Brilliant work. Massive step in the right direction."

Ben didn't know whether to be happy or pissed off – he settled for a little bit of both.

"Great," he said. "But next time, let me know."

"Of course. Always."

With that, Maria gave Ben a quick hug and fluttered into the theater. Ben looked up the block a final time. For a split second, he was sure he had him in his sights: A tallish man in a tweed coat was stepping lively down the street.

"Hello?" Ben called.

The man blinked. "Um, yes, hello...?"

Ben felt giddy. The man even had a British accent!

"I was wondering if you were..." With the words halfway out of his mouth, Ben stopped. No, up close, the nose was too big and the eyebrows too pronounced. "Sorry."

With a friendly nod, the man continued down the street, most likely off to see another show further down the block.

With a sigh, Ben glanced a final time up 45th Street, then turned toward the entrance. Maybe he'd find Richard after the show? Maybe he wouldn't show at all? Maybe he hadn't even seen Ben's post? In any case, it was time to head in.

"Lively crowd today," the ticket taker said as Ben moved inside. "Lots of parents with kids."

The ticket-taker was right. The lobby was brimming with families, some of them waiting for an usher to show them to their seats, some already on line at the concession stand. King had told Ben that merchandise or "merch" was where they would make a fortune. It seemed the old man knew what he was talking about. A display in the middle of the lobby was a shrine to the theatrical mercantile spirit. On sale were *Just Desserts* t-shirts, posters, roller-skates, apple pies, hats, gloves, souvenir booklets, and of course, the *Just Desserts* cast CD, recorded a week before the show and especially released at the time of previews. But what made Ben happiest was a copy of the book – his book – sitting smack in the center of the display: *The Worldwide Dessert*

Contest. Not only that, it was selling for a markup of $30 a copy!

Ben waved to the concessions lady. She winked back, ringing up a customer buying a pair of *Just Desserts'* socks.

"That'll be fifteen dollars," she said.

Smiling, Ben turned for the stairs. Things were looking better and better.

Like many old New York Theaters, the Imperial had a downstairs lounge with a bar, couches, and restrooms. Joining the line for the urinal, Ben found himself behind an angular man wearing a purple bowtie.

"It's about time Horatio King got back to work," the man remarked to a friend ahead of him on line. The friend was as squat as the first man was tall – together they reminded Ben of a modern-day Laurel and Hardy. Ben listened in.

"I know it," the friend said.

"A pretty strange topic for a musical, though," the first man said. "I hear there are flying crepes."

"Pies, actually," the second man said. "But it's gotta be better than *Black Hawk Down*, right?"

The angular man grinned widely. "I'll take flying desserts over dead bodies any day of the week."

The men laughed. Ben allowed himself a small smile. It was true. At the very least, *Just Desserts* had no body count. That was something.

By the time he reached the urinal, Ben found he had to pee more badly than he thought – nerves. He washed quickly and dried his hands, then headed back up to the lobby. Encouraged by the mad swirl of people – if anything, the lobby was now even more crowded – he took out his phone and wrote a text to the man himself.

At the theater. Good crowd.

A moment later, came the reply: *Good. I heard there was a rehearsal.*

Ben sighed. Was he the only one out of the loop? Before he could reply, King wrote again.

They fixed the fucking lights, I hope.

Ben wrote back: *And tweaked some performances apparently.*

No where to go but up. Good crowd, you say?

Sold out, I think.

Probably just want to see the old man fail. Got to go. A nurse is here with a device that looks shockingly like a cattle prod.

With the theater all but full, Ben decided to watch from the back. After saying a quick hello to the costume designer and the sound guy, he contented himself watching ushers bustle up and down the aisle, distributing Playbills, hurrying people to their seats. Then just before curtain, Ben noticed Everett Walker, jowls flapping, making his way down the opposite aisle. By his side was Natalie French, wearing a sensible skirt and blouse. With them was someone Ben didn't recognize, a pinched man with thinning blonde hair. For a second Ben wondered if it was Richard Sinclair. No, he was too young. Then he blinked and looked again. Was it Sven Nordgren? Who else could it be? Obviously, in town from his Icelandic writer's retreat. Ben shuddered. Had he been at that morning's rehearsal? Most probably. Ben considered pushing through the crowd to ask about it, then thought better of it. With the show about to begin and the theater nearly full there would be plenty of time to compare notes at intermission. As if on cue, the lights flickered. As last-minute stragglers were shown to their seats, Ben looked over the crowd.

"Hey, Dad?" a boy two rows down said. "Did I tell you? This show is going to have a pancake that turns into a giant trampoline."

The father laughed. "Where'd you hear that?"

"From the book. I told you that."

Ben nearly fell over. Was there really a family at the show because they were fans of his work as opposed to Horatio King's? It seemed hard to imagine, yet in this case, apparently true.

"Yes, you did," the father said with a laugh. "Also, what? The heroes fly to a land where people speak in rhymes?"

"Right," the boy said. "One of Applefeller's desserts is an apple soufflé and it puffs up into a giant balloon. So, they pump the soufflé full of helium and attach it to Applefeller's horse-drawn cart and fly it to visit Captain B. Rollie Ragoon."

"An apple soufflé balloon? Er, sounds interesting, son. I'm looking forward. Wonder how they're going to stage it."

Ben smiled. Maybe there were other kids who had dragged their parents to the show? Who knew? He looked over to Everett Walker and Sven to his right, chatting amiably. Then Ben looked over his shoulder a final time. For a moment he considered checking back outside to see if Richard Sinclair was waiting. But just then music director, Geneva Hickok, walked to the podium and took a bow to a smattering of light applause. No, Richard Sinclair would have to wait. The lights dimmed. When Geneva turned to the orchestra, Ben held his breath. Up went Geneva's arms. Down went the baton.

The main strain of "My Apple Pancake" filled the theater with a glorious sweep of strings. As the full orchestra segued into "The King of Dessert," the overture was off and running. Though he knew he shouldn't, Ben hummed along with each tune ("A Caramel Apple Stuck Upon my Face!") and even found himself dancing a bit to the lively strains of "Roller-Skating Apple Pies."

As the overture surged toward its finale, Ben pumped his fists. At the final stirring flourish, the crowd roared. Ben felt giddy. Maybe he had misjudged the show the night before? Maybe he had been nervous? The overture sure as hell sounded good anyway – and now as the scene changed to the opening, the lights seemed brighter. Ben could at least make out the dim outlines of John Applefeller at his bakery. As Applefeller's young assistant Samantha entered, the crowd applauded warmly. After a lively rendition of the opening number "The Man with the Changing Desserts," Applefeller and Samantha were left onstage, admiring a ten-foot-wide apple pancake.

SAMANTHA: It certainly is an unusual kind of dessert, isn't it, sir? How did you come up with it?

APPLEFELLER: Well, as my Aunt Harriet used to say, "When an apple dessert chef has lost for ten years in a row, then the world's largest apple pancake is what he should make."

SAMANTHA: Sounds logical to me, sir. After all, this apple pancake is too big to change. The ingredients are spread too far apart. In fact, I feel one hundred percent sure that this pancake will remain forever and always what it is – a pancake!

That was the cue for one of Ben's favorite songs in the show, the first he and King had written, "My Apple Pancake," the ballad where Applefeller sings of his deep desire to finally win the contest. But instead of the sweet strains of the violin section cuing the song, the lights darkened. Sylvester Sweet stepped out of the shadows, an unscripted appearance, at least as far as Ben was concerned. Sweet looked to the audience, laughed manically, then disappeared in a rush of blue dry ice.

"What the hell...?" Ben said to himself.

He looked over to Walker and Sven. Walker smiled, leaned toward Sven and whispered something to which Sven cracked the thinnest smile imaginable. Clearly, both men thought the addition a success. Is that what they had put in at that morning's rehearsal? Apparently so. Worse, the bright lights used in Scene One flickered away, giving the stage the dreary look of a second-rate production of *A Death of a Salesman*.

"Oh, Christ," Ben thought.

Even so, he waited patiently for the song he loved to begin. Instead, something altogether different happened. Geneva Hickok waved her arms, filling the theater with a cascade of minor. Horrified, Ben recognized the music immediately – the opening strains of "Dark Chocolate!"

"What the hell?"

This time Ben said it out loud. An usher and audience member looked his way and said "shhh!" at the same time, leaving Ben no choice but to bite his tongue and watch in shock. Instead of happily listening to a winsome love song to a giant apple pancake, Applefeller strutted downstage into a lone spotlight. Whose lyrics he sang, Ben didn't know for sure (probably Sven's) but they certainly weren't his. Not even his worst drafts were this bad. Shuddering, furious, Ben listened to Applefeller sing:

Dark Chocolate!
Unrefined and bitter!
Dark chocolate!
A baker's litter!
As it has to my self-worth

Let Chocolate rain down
And drown
The Earth!

Dark Chocolate!
Thou unholy sinner.
Dark Chocolate!
This year I'll be no winner.
As it has to my self-esteem
Let Chocolate
Keep percolating
Suffocating
My Dream!

Too stunned to compute more than a line or two of the rest of the lyric (which did, indeed, use Ben's rhyme of "shit" and "chocolate"), Ben watched mouth agape, unable to move. Not only was the song wholly inappropriate, it didn't make sense! But when the song mercifully ended with a melodramatic blackout, Ben saw Sven Nordgren jump to his feet, applauding wildly. As for the rest of the audience, they sat still, stunned, no doubt wondering what had happened to the perfectly pleasant well-lit show they had been watching. What had they had done to deserve a song such as this – one that bordered on the desperate ruminations of the suicidal? Some of the crowd had seen enough. During the scene change music, two sets of parents gathered their things (and children) and wandered, like bomb victims, up the aisle. Ben was seething. Yes, it was only previews – a time for experimentation – and yes, the show had gone badly the night before, but how dare Walker make such a change without consulting the authors!

But with the show lurching to the next scene at the dessert contest itself, Ben was trapped. Or was he? Furious, he looked to Sven and Walker. The two men were happily conspiring. How dare they take advantage of Horatio's illness to rewrite the show their way? How dare they cut a song without asking? How dare Sven write his own, plainly terrible, lyrics!

"Excuse me, sir," an usher said to Ben. "Where are you going?"

Ben was suddenly running full out. But not out the door. Not to find Richard Sinclair. No, he was running down the back of the lobby. Then as Scene Three began, he burst down the aisle. Dodging an usher, he accelerated into the orchestra section, took aim at Everett Walker, clenched his fists, and leapt.

19

Attack at the Imperial Theater
Special to the New York Post, April 12th
By Henry Twiddle

A shocking incident occurred during Act One of *Just Desserts*, the new Horatio King musical, this afternoon. Directly after the second song in the show, a ballad entitled "Dark Chocolate," King's collaborator and Broadway newcomer, Benjamin Willis, sprinted down the orchestra aisle and threw himself at director, Everett Walker.

"For a second I thought it was part of the act," said one patron after the show.

As did many audience members, especially when a fuming Mr. Willis tried to pick the larger Mr. Walker up over his head.

"I started applauding, to tell the truth," an elderly gentleman said. "So did everyone. I like that kind of theater. So raw."

Raw, yes, but unrehearsed. By the time ushers and security came pouring into the orchestra section, the audience realized that Mr. Willis's display wasn't part of the production. Applause turned to shocked gasps as Willis set on Nordgren next, pulling him by the tie into the aisle. According to witnesses, Willis eventually allowed himself to be led away after a short struggle, muttering, "My book! My beautiful book." As Walker and Nordgren were treated by medics in the lobby, assistant director Natalie French took to the stage to apologize for the interruption, whereupon the show resumed without incident.

As of this writing, Mr. Wills was being taken to the 101st Precinct for booking. There is no concrete motive behind the young writer's attack, though one suspects some sort of intra-show vendetta. Walker and Nordgren have not said whether they intend to press charges, but producer Maria Feltenstein told the press that Ben Willis would no longer be welcome at rehearsals or previews until the situation was satisfactorily resolved.

"I applaud the American passion for the arts," Ms. Feltenstein said. "But I draw the line at interrupting a performance."

Willis's absence, if it holds up, will put *Just Desserts* in great jeopardy. With famed composer Horatio King in the hospital recovering from a heart attack, the show must now maneuver the stormy seas of previews without the authors present.

"It's highly unusual," said Emily Brancroft, head of the Dramatists' Guild, by phone. "Previews are when writers make changes and tweak the show, preparing for opening night. With one of the writers in the ICU and another with a possible restraining order, well, that's going to make things difficult."

To make matters worse, audience response after the show was not positive. Complaints ranged from poor lighting choices to bombastic lyrics. One patron complained of being overcome by a profusion of dry ice. If producers were concerned, they didn't show it.

"Mark my words," Maria Feltenstein said. "*Just Desserts* is going to be a hit."

Sources note that both Everett Walker and Sven Nordgren were treated for minor injuries at the theater and released.

20

"He should be back soon, don't you think?"

Ben looked at his phone. It was quarter to five.

"Well, the matinee ended ten minutes ago."

The two collaborators were in King's hospital room, where the old man was still convalescing. A week after what the theater community was calling "the incident," the article in the Post had been followed by others in the Times, Playbill, Newsday, Broadway.com, and a litany of theater blogs, all describing their take on Ben's mental lapse and subsequent restraining order. Now the collaborators were waiting for a report on the show from none other than Richard Sinclair. To Ben's surprise, it had been Richard – not his mother – who had bailed him out of the 101st precinct after the attack.

"I followed you here, old boy," the man had said. "I had a feeling that Horatio would've wanted me to."

Once he was free, Ben had taken the British gentleman directly to the hospital. With virtually no period of awkwardness, the two men had fallen back into a fast friendship, then something that Ben saw was more. Now Richard was doing them the ultimate favor: seeing the show. Though King and Ben had heard reports from loyal cast members and colleagues from the AMI workshop that the production was in a state of outrageous flux, they were dying for a direct report from a trusted friend. Of course, bloggers were still a source of the show's basic progress.

"Look at this," King said, holding his computer in his lap.

"*SeesEverything* says there are now two reprises of 'Dark Chocolate.'"

Ben shuddered. "Two?"

"Yes, two," King said. He read further down the page. "Damn."

"What?"

"And *BroadwayFreakazoid* says they cut 'King of Dessert.'"

"King of Dessert?" Ben said. "That's one of the best. Why?"

"Doesn't say. Maybe Everett Walker found it too tuneful."

"I thought you told him not to change anything without telling you," Ben exclaimed.

"I did."

"Then what the hell is he doing? Where are Michelle Marks and the other producers?"

"Fuck if I know," King said. "Without you and me to reign him in, Walker is a wild man. Don't forget. This is the man who staged *Hamlet* in outer space."

Ben shook himself. "I know. Don't remind me."

The two friends – for that's what they now were in their own strange way – were silent for a short moment. Then King shook his head and laughed.

"What?" Ben asked. "Is something about this funny?"

"Actually, yes," King said. "Your attack at the theater. I still can't believe that you tried to pick Walker up. He's not a small man."

Ben had to smile, too. What else could he do at this point?

"I was a little bit pissed, I guess."

"You think?"

"Okay, really pissed," Ben said.

"What were some of those lyrics to their version of 'Dark

Chocolate' again?"

"I blocked them out," Ben said. "Something about drowning in it."

"How light-hearted," King said.

"Yeah," Ben said. "Really upbeat."

"Where do you stand with the restraining order?" King asked.

Ben stretched. "My mom's lawyer is working on it. I have a hearing in a few days."

King stroked his beard. Though still sick, he was clearly on the mend. His color was back to normal, his telltale energy returning.

"Well, I hope your lawyer knows what she's doing," King said. "We need one of us at the theater. And soon, too. According to these blogs, the show is barely recognizable. Next thing we know, Sven is going to translate it into Norwegian."

Just then, the door burst open. In stepped Richard Sinclair. A lanky, elegant man, he was dressed in a sports coat and slacks. His beard was closely trimmed, his mustache combed.

"Well, well?" King asked. "How was it?"

Without saying a word, Richard took King's hand and gave him a kiss on the cheek.

"First things first. How are you, my darling?"

King smiled warmly. Ben grinned. It was nice to see.

"Will you look at this, Ben?" King asked. "I've got a handsome Englishman by my side once again."

"I see," Ben said.

"And as much as I hate to admit it, I owe it all to you, my boy."

Ben shrugged. "Not really."

"Yes, really." King squeezed Richard's hand. "You got in

touch with him. You reached out. You forced me to come to that blasted workshop so I got hash things out with Ethan. You paved the way."

"We both thank you," Richard said with a small bow.

"Okay," Ben said. He smiled. "I'll take some of the credit. But you two would've found each other anyway."

"Not necessarily," King said. "Don't tell me you've already forgotten what a stubborn, uncivilized fuck I can be?"

Ben laughed. "Well, true."

"Anyway," King said. "Enough about the love life of a desiccated old man." He turned to Richard. "Tell us everything. How's the show?"

Ben steeled himself for the worst, hoping that what he had heard wasn't true. Of course, he knew deep down that it most certainly was. He had gone to the theater a few times over the past week. But even from one hundred feet down 45th Street – the closest he was legally allowed to Everett Walker and Sven – it was evident how badly it was going. Audience members poured out at the end with barely a smile between them then dispersed quickly into the night as though they had witnessed a tale of the great purges of Eastern Europe as opposed to a light-hearted romp about a dessert contest.

"We hear there are now two reprises of 'Dark Chocolate,'" Ben said.

Richard grimaced. "Try three."

"Three?" King said. He sat up in his bed.

"Yes," Richard said. "Applefeller sings it twice and his assistant once."

"Samantha?" Ben said. "She's a ten-year-old girl!"

"Does she rhyme 'shit' with 'chocolate'?" King asked.

Richard nodded. "I caught 'dimwit' as well." He sighed.

"Also 'tit.'"

"Tit?" King said. "Jesus!"

Richard sat on the side of the bed and took King's hand. Ben was impressed by their easy comfort together.

"Are you sure you want me to go on?" Richard asked.

King shuddered. "Is it that bad?"

"I'm afraid so."

Ben sighed. "You might as well tell us."

"How were the other lyrics?" King asked. "Have they changed more of them?"

"Frankly," Richard said. "At times they were bloody difficult to understand."

"Why?" Ben asked. "Because the sound was bad?"

"No," Richard said, standing up. "Because an occasional verse was in Norwegian."

King and Ben exchanged a glance.

"Norwegian?" King exclaimed.

"You said that a minute ago," Ben said.

"Yes, as a joke!"

"No joke, I'm afraid," Richard said. "One of the ushers confirmed it for me at intermission. Apparently, she researched it."

"Christ!" King said. "What a fucking time to have a heart attack. What else? Go on. Don't hold back."

"How were the lights?" Ben asked. "Were they bright?"

Richard stroked his beard. "If you like graveyards at midnight, then yes."

"How about Judge Barkle?" King asked. "Did the caramel apple at least get some laughs?"

Richard shook his head. "I'm afraid not."

"What?" Ben asked.

"Don't tell me it's stuck to his crotch now," King said.

"No, it's on his face all right…"

"Then what's the problem?" King asked.

"As the show progresses, you see, the audience comes to discover that the apple isn't an apple at all."

"Not an apple?" Ben said. "What is it then?"

Richard paused, Ben thought for dramatic effect.

"A hand grenade."

Ben and King exchanged a long, distressed glance.

"A hand grenade?" King said. "What the hell!"

"Does it go off?" Ben asked.

Richard shook his head. "No, thankfully."

"Well, that's something, I suppose," King said. "That didn't work so well in *Black Hawk Down*."

"No one dies then?" Ben said. "That's a relief."

Richard wagged a finger. "Ah, ha! Not so fast."

"What?" Ben asked. "Someone dies?"

Richard nodded. "Dentina."

"Dentina?" King yelled. He was so upset he nearly sprang out of bed. "She's the fucking ingénue!"

"Imagine my surprise," Richard said.

"How did it happen?" Ben asked.

"Sylvester Sweet," Richard began.

"Her brother killed her?" King interrupted.

"In a giant hot fudge concoction."

Ben couldn't believe it. "Drowned her in it?"

Richard nodded. "She's sort of baked into it, you see, in a big production dance number, leaving the audience to assume that she suffocates."

King and Ben exchanged another glance.

"We have to get to that theater," King said.

"How?" Ben said. "You're sick, and I'm a felon. Everett Walker will never let me in the door."

"Not if he isn't there, he won't," King said.

"What?"

"I'm a co-producer. The majority shareholder, in fact."

Richard nodded. "Quite right."

"So what are you saying?" Ben asked. "You have the right to fire Everett and Sven?"

"Should have done it a week ago, yet I was hoping I could give notes from bed and that he wouldn't go off the deep end."

"Then who'll take over?" Ben asked.

King smiled. "How about Walker's assistant?"

"Natalie?" Ben said. "Really?"

"I should've listened to you when you first brought it up," King said. "It'll be her big break, and all she'll have to do is reinstate the show the way it was and light the damned thing. She should be able to handle that. The dance captain can help with the choreography."

"That's great," Ben said. "But you're sick. Forgive me for saying it, but you nearly died a week ago."

"True enough," King said.

"Perhaps you shouldn't risk it," Richard said.

"Oh, no?" King said. "Listen, Richard, darling."

Ben blinked. Had King just used the word 'darling?'

"Yes?"

King took Richard's hand and held it tenderly.

"It's been a wonderful week with you back in my life. I hope it's many more years. But I am a man of the theater! If I am meant to die, it might as well be saving this show. Or trying to anyway. I owe it to myself. Christ, I owe it to Ben! Now, my wheelchair!"

"Really?" Ben asked.

With that, King lurched from the bed, placed his feet on the floor, and stood for the first time in a week.

"Unplug me," he cried.

"Really, now, Horatio," Richard said. "Let's talk this over."

"Unplug me!"

Ben and Richard exchanged a glance. Richard shrugged. Ben pulled the wires attached to the heart monitor away from King's chest.

"My IV," King said.

"No," Richard said. "We take that along and that's final."

King nodded. "Okay, we take the IV. Now my phone."

Ben handed King his cell as the old man allowed Richard to help him to the side of his bed.

"Who you calling?" Ben asked.

King didn't answer. Instead, he punched a contact and pressed "Send." A moment later, someone answered.

"Hello there? Yes, King here. Good. Glad it's going well, Everett. Yes, excellent…Today's matinee was a success? A darker, more beautiful version of the story? Excellent. I love it. It's glorious. Except for one thing… GET THE FUCK OUT OF MY THEATER AND TAKE YOUR CRAZY ASS NORWEGIAN WITH YOU! YOU'RE FIRED!"

King hung up.

Ben gasped. Richard laughed.

"What?" King said. "Wasn't I clear enough?"

21

PLAYBILL – April 18th
Carnage at the Imperial

The troubled production of Horatio King's *Just Desserts* grew bumpier yesterday in an unheard of round of firings one week before opening. Though details are sketchy, sources close to the production say that the great composer checked himself out of New York Hospital, where he was recovering from a heart attack, at approximately five-thirty p.m., and arrived at the theater a half an hour later in the company of his young collaborator, Ben Willis (previously detained for assault), and famed actor Richard Sinclair. Reportedly, King and crew found Everett Walker and dramaturg Sven Nordgren in the orchestra section giving notes to the cast – this though King had already fired Walker over the phone. According to several witnesses, King thundered down the orchestra aisle in a wheelchair, nearly impaling the British director on his IV. After King delivered what one observer called "an explicative-peppered rant," Walker vacated the premises with Nordgren in tow.

"We will revert to the version of the show we had two weeks ago," King announced to a cheering cast. 'Dark Chocolate' is cut! All small fire arms are cut! All lines will be in English! Dentina will live! We have one week. Let's do this!"

King then confirmed that Natalie French has been put in charge of the production. She told *Playbill*, "I'm thrilled to be working with Horatio King and Ben Willis to make *Just Desserts* the sweetest possible concoction." Though unable to be reached for comment, Walker was seen last night boarding a plane back to London, where he is slated to begin work in a month's time on a production of *All My Sons* lit entirely in periwinkle. As for Sven Nordgren, word has it that he is on its way to Outer Mongolia to regroup by Genghis Khan's grave.

Just Desserts is slated to open on Broadway on April 26th.

22

It was opening night. Ben sat in a small office off the stage door wearing his only suit, a blue one he had bought to graduate from college.

"This is so exciting," Gretchen said. She and Amy had come down from Vermont to attend the opening. "Who'd have thought that Ben Willis, the kid I met freshman year, would get a show on Broadway?"

"And with Horatio King, no less," Amy said.

Ben smiled. "Hard to believe, right?"

"You must feel amazing," Amy said.

It was a good feeling. No, a great feeling. A once-in-a-lifetime thrill. But along with the thrill came a healthy dose of opening night jitters, worse due to the frenetic pace of the previous week's rehearsals. It hadn't been all that hard to reinstate the original script, but rewrites and tweaks still proved necessary, leaving King and Ben a week's time to do work that had been allotted nearly a month. Fixing the lights alone took two full days of tech. A new choreographer was promoted from the chorus to massage the dance numbers. The caramel apple was no longer weaponized. The ballad "My Apple Pancake" was reinstated to its rightful spot in the show. Still, in keeping with theatrical tradition, the previous day's final preview had been a disaster. Curtains had refused to open, the giant apple pancake was late rolling onto the stage, the actor playing the Ragoon had stumbled over his cleverest rhymes. Most alarming, however, were the roller-skating apple pies. These moving desserts had remained stationary, necessitating a group of stage hands to rush from the wings to push them.

Now with everything fixed – hopefully – it was now or never. While most shows receive critics during the tail end of previews, due to the unique problems plaguing *Just Desserts*, major reviewers agreed to put off attending until opening. Which meant that the theater was now filling up with critics from every paper in the city, from the *Times* to the *News* to the more obscure. The PR department had told Ben they expected a reviewer from a new paper called the *Soho Manifesto*. It made sense. It wasn't every day that a new Horatio King musical opened on Broadway.

Gretchen took Ben's hand.

"Listen," she said. "Whatever happens tonight and tomorrow in the press, this is a big win for you, right?"

"Huge," Amy said.

Ben swallowed. He knew it was true. But now that he had come this far, he needed the show to be a hit. He didn't think he could stand a flop.

"I suppose," Ben said. "Right now, I'm a little bit too close to it."

"Hey," Amy said. "You got to hang out with Horatio King. In my book, that's amazing."

Ben nodded again. Yes, that was amazing. In truth, that had been the best part of the process, being a collaborator with that strangely profane, lovable man.

"Anyway," Gretchen said. "We got you an opening night gift."

She nodded to Amy, who took a wrapped package out of her bag.

"What is it?" Ben asked.

"Open it," Amy said.

Ben did as he was told. Crumpled wrapping was soon on the floor, and Ben was holding a framed, laminated caramel apple with the words OPENING NIGHT, JUST DESSERTS engraved on the bottom in bold print.

Ben laughed. "Oh, my God. Thanks."

"Just make sure to hang it on a wall," Gretchen said. "Not on your face."

"I will," Ben said. "I love it."

He suddenly felt acutely lonely. Gretchen and Amy seemed so happy together. So did everyone for that matter. Mo was in England with Nate. Over the past month, Ben's sole contact had been with people at the theater. Though Ben had found himself liking Natalie more and more, admiring her sharp wit and unflappable calm under pressure, a discrete inquiry revealed that she was all but engaged.

"Anyway," Ben said. "Thanks."

He hugged them both, first separately, then together.

"So what do we do now?" Gretchen asked.

"I think the time has come," Ben said. "You guys take your seats and I go outside to meet and greet a little bit."

"Cool," Amy said.

"We're proud of you, Ben," Gretchen said.

"Yep," Amy agreed.

Ben hugged them again. For some reason – he wasn't quite sure why – he felt like crying. Already that day, he had received over two hundred emails and texts from relatives and old and new friends.

"Hey," Gretchen said. "You okay?"

Ben nodded. "Fine. Just overwhelmed, I guess. Everybody's been so nice."

"Well, lots of people love you," Gretchen said.

Ben nodded, trying to take it in. "Thanks for the gift. See you soon, okay?"

"Okay. After the show."

As they left, Ben hated to admit that Gretchen and Amy looked good together. They made sense as a couple. With a sigh, he looked in the mirror, straightened his tie, and headed out the stage door. As he stepped onto 45th Street, a limo was pulling up in front of the theater. Someone he didn't recognize posed for a few pictures, then went inside. A split second later, someone Ben did recognize, a short man with a tightly trimmed mustache and severe frown, hustled past and turned into the theater.

"Shit," Ben whispered to himself.

It was Edgar Childs, chief theater critic for *The New York Times*.

Ben said a little prayer to the theater Gods, as Harrison, his now ex-roommate, and Justin waved from the entrance. The couple had just moved into a studio in Fort Greene.

"Break a leg!" Harrison called.

Ben smiled.

"I'll do my best! See you after?"

"You know it."

And as Ben's friends found their way inside, another limo pulled up to the theater. This time Ben recognized the occupants. Out stepped Horatio King and Richard Sinclair, both in tuxedos. King had trimmed his beard for the occasion. He leaned easily on his cane. Richard was wearing a navy bowler hat. A crowd of on-lookers applauded.

"Ben," King called.

"Horatio," Ben called back as a reporter, a young woman in a black skirt and yellow blouse, waved him over.

"Let's have a few words with the authors, shall we?"

Ben felt someone else – another reporter probably – grab his arm and direct him to King's side.

"Hello there, my boy," the old man said. "Ready for the bigtime?"

Ben smiled. "I think so."

"Good."

By that time, the reporter was facing her cameraman.

"This is Amanda Sparks from Broadway.com and I'm outside the Imperial Theater with Horatio King and Ben Willis, authors of the new musical *Just Desserts*."

With that brief intro, she turned to Ben.

"Let's start with you, Mr. Willis. What's it been like to work with musical theater's preeminent living composer?"

Ben looked to King and smiled.

"Careful," King said.

"As you might imagine," Ben said, "it's been wonderful."

"And how does it feel to have your first Broadway show?"

"The first of many," King cut in.

Ben blushed. "Well, I don't know about that…but it feels awesome." He smiled. "As long as the apple pies roller-skate when they're supposed to, everything will be fine."

"Yes," the reporter said, looking at her notes. "The blogosphere has been lighting up with news of your show. Technical difficulties, right? Two nights ago, your flying pies nearly took off someone's head in the balcony."

King laughed. "You might say one of our audience members got a nice little haircut for the price of their ticket. But all of that is under control now."

The reporter nodded. "Controversy surrounding this production has been no secret. Everett Walker was fired a short week ago."

"Because he was an idiot," King stated.

"Oh, really?" the reporter replied. "Is that a little bit harsh?"

"Not harsh enough, actually," King said. "Everett Walker is a genius but imposed a ridiculous conception upon our show. He needed to be removed."

"Okay then," the reporter said to the camera. "You heard it here, theater fans. Everett Walker: genius idiot." She turned back to King. "How has the rehearsal process been since promoting Natalie French?"

"Natalie is a superstar," King said. "The best thing she did was revert the lyrics back to English. After that, it was smooth enough sailing."

"One last thing," the reporter said. "Mr. King. This is your first show since your most infamous flop, *Black Hawk Dawn*. How does it feel to be back on Broadway?"

King smiled. To Ben's surprise, he took his hand.

"These past six months have been among the most pleasurable in my career," he said. "This whole experience has been a rare out-of-nowhere gift. And I owe it to this young man here, Ben Willis."

Ben gasped, amazed.

"All right then," the reporter said. "Best of luck to you all." Then to the camera. "That was the great Horatio King, ladies and gentlemen."

Ben walked toward the theater but was intercepted.

"Ben!"

He wheeled around. Cutting through the crowd were Johnny Framingham, Billy Hansen, and Jen Rosenthal.

"You guys came!"

Jen gave Ben a hug.

"Wouldn't miss it. This is your Broadway opening."

"Hey," Billy said. "If you can do it, then it makes us think that maybe we can, too."

"Right," Johnny said. "You're our inspiration."

"Mine, too," a voice said.

Ben turned to see Ethan Hancock stepping out of the crowd. He was holding hands with a good-looking man with silver hair.

"You know my husband, Jacques."

Ben nodded. "I do now. Nice to meet you."

"A pleasure," Jacques said. "And congratulations."

"And to you, too," Ethan called across the crowd to Horatio. King smiled back, broadly.

"Ethan! Thank you. You remember Richard?"

Suddenly, Ethan did something Ben had never seen before – he blushed.

"I don't know if we ever met…not officially anyway."

"We didn't," Richard said, then ever the gentleman, added: "But a pleasure to meet you now."

With that, Richard extended his hand. Ethan took it. They shook awkwardly.

"Break legs," Ethan said to Horatio and Ben, in a hurry to move on. "See you after."

With that, Ethan, Jacques, Jen, Johnny, and Billy went inside. Watching them go, Ben felt another wave of loneliness. His Broadway opening and everyone seemed to have someone except him. In fact, a day earlier he had succumbed to the inevitable and agreed to sit with his mom. But just as he was turning to go into the theater, he felt a hand on his shoulder. It was Horatio King.

"Don't look so glum, my boy," the old man said.

Ben shook himself. "I'm not, just taking it all in."

"Bullshit," King said. "You're depressed."

"I am?"

"Yes, but that's good. It means you're growing up. Now follow me."

"What's going on?" Ben said.

King and Richard exchanged a bemused glance.

"Let's just say that one good turn deserves another," Richard said.

"Precisely so."

Ben looked into the theater. The two old men were grinning full out now.

"Wait," Ben said, picking up on it. "Is there someone…?"

He stopped, realizing how happy the thought made him. For a split second he thought that Gretchen had sent Amy packing and that she was on a bus back to Vermont and her baby already. But then he realized.

"You bastard," he said.

King laughed. "I suppose I am. But no more than you were to me. Well, what are you waiting for? Get your ass inside the theater and find your date. And I'll give you a hint. It's not a raccoon."

Ben felt his grin transform into a full-fledged grin. For the first time all day, he felt truly happy. Turning, he walked briskly into the theater, maneuvering his way through the thick of the opening crowd, past the concessions stand, past the first aisle down the orchestra to the second. There his heart dropped. Standing by the aisle was…his mother? She gave him a kiss on the cheek, then wiped away the lipstick.

"Mom," he stammered. "I thought you were…"

"Shut up," she said. "I'm not your seatmate, dear. But I am so proud of you."

Ben gave her a quick hug and looked down the aisle. Before he could say another word, his mother gave him a push.

"Go. She's down there."

So Ben went, wending his way down the aisle, accepting congratulations along the way, walking faster and faster until – there! – he saw her, seated fourth row, center, looking his way, short hair, red lipstick, and light blue eyes.

"Mo," he said, still slightly stunned. "You're back."

Mo grinned. "Somebody sent me a ticket. Said you needed a date."

Ben glanced up the aisle and caught King's eye. The old man flashed a thumbs up. Ben mouthed, "thank you."

"So are you going to sit down?" Mo asked. "I hear there are roller-skating apple pies."

"Roller-skating apple pies?" Ben said. "Sounds absurd."

Mo smiled more broadly. "That's what I thought. We can make fun of it together."

He laughed and slipped into the aisle seat.

"So where's the famous Gretchen?" Mo asked.

Ben looked over his shoulder. The couple was three rows back.

"Sitting there with the famous Amy."

Mo smiled. "That's a story I have to hear sometime."

"Yes, sometime," Ben said. "Where's Nate?"

Mo smiled. "Who's Nate?"

"So he's history? On Instagram you two looked pretty happy."

Mo's eyes went wide. "Oh, so you've been checking up on me."

Ben shrugged. "A little."

"Then you might have noticed that he was usually the one

posting, not me."

"So it's over?"

Mo nodded. "Put it this way. I am using him as the basis for a character in my dystopia. But don't worry. I'm killing him off."

Ben laughed. "Have him eaten by a polar bear."

"Are you still writing that story?"

"Maybe," Ben said. "Once I have the time."

"You should."

Mo leaned forward and gave Ben a light kiss.

"By the way, congratulations. I'm so glad I'm here."

"Me, too," Ben said.

With that, the lights began to dim. Geneva Hickok walked onto the podium to a large wave of applause. Ben kissed Mo back then settled into his chair. A spotlight shone on Geneva. She raised her arm and the crowd went still. Ben held his breath for a split second. This was it – his Broadway opening – win or lose he would have this moment forever.

"Here we go," Mo whispered.

"Yeah," Ben said, forcing himself to believe it. "Here we go."

Geneva swept down the baton. The overture began.

23

"Hard to believe he won, isn't it?"

Ben nodded. "Yep. Crazy."

"He's not even that good. The goddamned apple does all the work."

It was June. After a slate of reviews that ranged from raves to pans – some critics had been charmed by the show's sweetness, others disgusted by it – *Just Desserts* had won exactly one Tony Award: Jack Shore as Judge Nathaniel Barkle for Best Supporting Actor in a Musical.

Now Ben was in his usual spot in King's living room on the sofa.

"At least you got your nomination," King said. "Best book in a musical."

"Yep," Ben said.

King chuckled. "It's still hard to believe you lost to a script about a bunch of dogs."

Ben nodded. "Yeah, that sort of hurt."

Indeed, for all the criticism endured in the AMI workshop, *Dalmatians* had swept most of the major awards, including Best Musical. Sir Sanabelle had even nudged King out for best score.

"And I still can't believe that rock 'n roll writing monstrosity beat me for best music," the old man said.

To that, Juniper jumped on his lap and licked his face. King, as was his wont, pushed him to the floor – but gently.

"Tony voters are morons," Ben noted.

"Yes," King said. He smiled. "Except when they vote for me."

Ben nodded. He was beginning to learn that was also true of reviewers. The ones who liked the show, he loved; the ones who hated it, he returned in kind. Especially Edgar Childs. The *Times'* headline had read: *"When Sickly Sweet Goes Sour."* It had taken Ben a full month to get over the sheer vitriol of the review before he could let it go. But critics, he soon learned, had little to do with whether a show was going to stay open. That had to do with one thing only: ticket sales.

"So?" Ben began, after a pause.

"Yes?" King said. Then he laughed. "Okay, ask it. You want to know if we're going to run."

Ben swallowed, embarrassed. Was he that easy to read? "Well, yeah. I mean, now that the Tonys are over?"

It was a critical question. Despite the wacky family-friendly subject matter – or perhaps because of it – ticket sales had been only middling. Kid-friendly matinees and weekend nights were packed while Tuesday, Wednesday, and Thursday nights were decidedly not.

King shrugged. "If we can get through the summer, next fall should pick up. Our word of mouth is good, but our show is pretty expensive, what with all the special effects."

Ben nodded. "Roller-skating pies don't come cheap."

"No, they don't. Those wheels are expensive."

The two men were silent for a minute.

"But you know, Ben, don't worry about it."

Ben was surprised. "What? Don't worry if the show is going to run or not?"

King stroked his beard and gave Juniper a little scratch. "Shows comes and go, but you know what? Hell, you've got your girl now and that's what's important."

Ben smiled. "That's true. But I'd like them both."

"Sometimes we can't be that greedy," King said.

Ben sighed. "I guess."

"I do like her," King said. "Your girl."

"Mo?" Ben said. "Me, too."

King wagged a finger in his direction. "No, my boy. You love her."

Ben blushed. It was true. He had uttered the words a week earlier.

"I knew it!" King went on. "I always said you'd do well with a nice Catholic."

"She's Presbyterian, remember?"

"Whatever. With a goy then."

"Thanks, so far so good," Ben said.

Actually, it was better than that. Ben felt so strongly he had already entertained fantasies of Mo moving in, perhaps to a new apartment, one without rats or raccoons.

"And you and Richard?" Ben asked. "When do you leave for your trip?"

"In a week," King said. "Though I'm worried Rome will be too hot."

"Good food, though," Ben said.

"Yes," King replied. "And some good alone time with my seventy-year-old boy-toy. Again, I have you to thank."

"Likewise," Ben said. "I don't know what I would've done about Mo if you hadn't intervened."

King chuckled. "Richard's idea, of course, but I backed him up on it right away."

"She's talented, by the way," Ben said. "Her first book made me cry. Actual tears."

"For the right reasons, I hope," King said.

"Yes, it was. It was touching."

"Good for her then," King said. "Are you working on a book now?"

"Maybe," Ben said. "If you can believe it, I have an idea about a polar bear who's a baseball genius. At least that's what I think it'll be about. Once I have an outline, I have to talk about it with my editor."

"Ah, the famed Eleanor Crumb," King said.

"Right."

Now it was King's turn to pause, uncomfortably.

"What?" Ben asked.

"Well," King said. "I was really wondering…Any musical ideas?"

Ben shook his head. "Not really…why?"

King sighed then said as almost an afterthought. "That's all right. After vacation maybe we can find one."

Ben blinked. "Find one? You mean, you and me?"

King looked almost embarrassed. "I mean, you are interested, aren't you? In writing another, right? I'm almost eighty-six but not a corpse yet. I still have energy enough to write music. I have it in me if you do."

Ben nodded. "Oh, yes. I do, absolutely."

To that, Juniper barked twice.

King laughed. "The mutt approves. I guess that seals it."

"I guess it does."

An awkward pause. Neither man knew quite what to say, both slightly embarrassed at admitting they wanted their collaboration to continue.

"Anyway," King said. "Richard is coming over soon, so you'd better clear out."

Ben smiled. "On my way."

King laughed. "Don't make me throw another Tony Award at you."

"I won't. I'm going. Hey, have a good trip."

"I will," King said. "I'll text you pictures."

"Do that."

"Say hi to your girl for me."

"I will."

To that, the old man took Ben's hand and gave it a squeeze.

"Good work on the show. Whatever happens, we have that in our back pocket."

"Right," Ben said. "Thanks."

"No, thank you." King smiled. "Now get the fuck out."

And so Ben did. With a quick goodbye, he walked out into the warm New York City air. He had to meet Mo for dinner but had time to kill. He could go to a bookstore to browse and read or to a Starbucks to think and write. Instead, Ben set out for Times Square. After all, it was a Saturday, almost time for the matinee audience to hit 45th Street after the show. Given uneven ticket sales, Ben had no idea how long *Just Desserts* would last – maybe not even through the summer. Would it hurt to wander by as the show was getting out to take another look for the memory banks?

A cab pulled lazily around the corner. To Ben's surprise, an ad for *Just Desserts* was on its side. It seemed like fate. He wasn't rich but he was making some money now. Why not travel in style?

"Taxi," Ben called.

The cab pulled to a stop. Ben opened the door and slid in.

"Where to?" the driver asked.

"Over to Times Square. 45th Street please."

The driver started the meter and nudged the gas.

"Times Square, huh? Lots of shows open now. Seeing anything?"

Ben thought about the matinee crowd of parents and kids that would be streaming happily out of the theater. Then he thought of his name on the marquee and the fans waiting eagerly by the stage door.

"Seeing anything?" he said with a smile. "I sure am."

Curtain